SAXBY SMART
PRIVATE DETECTIVE

The
*Saxby Smart
Private Detective*
series:

Find fun features, exclusive mysteries
and much more at:

www.saxbysmart.co.uk

Find out more at:
www.simoncheshire.co.uk

SAXBY SMART
PRIVATE DETECTIVE

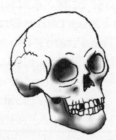

Secret
of the
Skull

SIMON CHESHIRE

Piccadilly Press • London

To Constable Cheshire (1937-2010)
who told many a detective story.

First published in Great Britain in 2010
by Piccadilly Press Ltd,
5 Castle Road, London NW1 8PR
www.piccadillypress.co.uk

A catalogue record for this book is available
from the British Library

ISBN: 978 1 84812 055 6 (paperback)

3 5 7 9 10 8 6 4

Printed and bound by CPI Group (UK) Ltd, Croydon, CR0 4YY
Cover design and illustration by Patrick Knowles

Mixed Sources
Product group from well-managed
forests and other controlled sources
www.fsc.org Cert no. TT-COC-002227
© 1996 Forest Stewardship Council
FSC

Introduction:
Important Facts

My name is Saxby Smart and I'm a private detective. I go to St Egbert's School, my office is in the garden shed, and this is the eighth book of my case files. Unlike some detectives, I don't have a sidekick, so that part I'm leaving up to you – pay attention, I'll ask questions.

CASE FILE TWENTY-TWO:

SECRET
OF THE
SKULL

CHAPTER
ONE

SCOTLAND YARD, LONDON. FBI HEADQUARTERS, Washington DC. Saxby Smart's Crime HQ, my garden shed. Three major centres of crime-busting operations. But which is the odd one out?

The answer is: my garden shed. Reason: because the other two have got heating systems, and my bloomin' shed hasn't. During the coldest months of the year, instead of concentrating on being a brilliant schoolboy detective, I have to concentrate on having enough blankets and woolly hats in the shed to stop me from shivering while I'm working on case notes.

It's not fair. I bet Inspector Whatever-Name of the Yard never has this trouble! The only thing I like about the winter is that at least I'm free of hayfever for a few months.

I was shivering in my shed the day I was asked for help by a kid in my year group at St Egbert's School who we always call The Skull. It was a Sunday afternoon, and I was wrapped up in a thick blanket, nestled in my Thinking Chair (the battered old leather armchair where I do all my detective-type thinking).

I was busy going through my notebook and writing up some observations on *The Case of the Shrinking Monkey*. It had been a long but fairly routine investigation, so I won't bore you with the details of it here. I was rapidly sliding into a bad mood, partly because of the cold and partly because the thick woollen gloves I was wearing meant the pen kept slipping out of my fingers. I glanced up at the tall, teetering piles of gardening and DIY stuff I'm forced to share the shed with. You'd think whopping great piles of junk would at least act as insulation, wouldn't you? But no, apparently not.

There was a knock on the shed door and a voice called out, 'Hello? Anyone at home?'

'Come in!' I called back. 'Welcome to the South Pole – mind out for the penguins!'

An icy blast of air sliced through the shed as the door opened and The Skull came in. Calling him The Skull makes him sound like he had a black cloak and an evil cackle, but Peter Skulyevic (pronounced skull-ee-ay-vitch) was just a regular kid. I'd walk to school with him sometimes, as he lived only one street away from me. He tramped into the shed wearing a chunky hooded anorak to which a number of damp leaves were sticking, and fleece-lined boots which had clearly been soaking up icy puddles for an hour or two.

Everyone called him The Skull – or simply Skull, or occasionally Jack *Skull*-ington – for two reasons. Firstly, because Skulyevic is so unusual and long it was just crying out to be nicknamed. Secondly, because of his equally unusual head. It was rather domed, and his hair was perfectly flat, and the impression you got when you looked at him was . . . well, very skull-like.

It was a terribly unfortunate coincidence of name and looks. What made the effect worse was the way he appeared to have a permanent smirk on his face. He was one of those people who seem to be about to laugh out loud, or start giggling about something, for no reason.

He could drive teachers barmy. 'Perhaps you'd like to share the joke with the rest of the class?' they'd demand, or 'Have I said something funny?' To which he would innocently reply, 'No. Honestly.' And then he'd look like he was smirking all over again.

Nice guy. Very good at model trains.

'Here, you can sit in my Thinking Chair,' I said, shifting my stuff over on my desk so I could sit on it. 'Do you want a blanket?'

'No, I'm fine,' he smirked. 'I think it's rather cosy in here.' He settled back in the chair.

'Now then,' I said, 'how can I help you? I have the feeling that you've only come here as a last resort. You've been making your own investigations? Perhaps secretly tailing a suspect this afternoon?'

He stared at me. 'But . . . Yes! How could you possibly know that?'

I'd made an educated guess based on three things: the freezing weather, his appearance and where he lived. Have you worked out what I'd been thinking?

'It's a very cold day today,' I said. 'Not many people are going to be out and about longer than they need to be. You live only one street away from here, so you could reach this shed in a matter of minutes. But your boots have clearly been soaking up puddles for quite a while. You've been out for ages.

'The fact that all those wet leaves are sticking to your coat implies you've been around a lot of foliage too. Been gardening? Hardly, in this weather. I know something's going on, that you've got some kind of problem, otherwise you wouldn't be here. So perhaps you've picked up all those leaves while trying to stay out of sight? Behind hedges or trees? Why would you want to stay hidden? So that someone doesn't spot you.'

He scratched his round head. 'Yes, well, when you put it like that, it's very simple, really.'

'Who is it you've been following?' I asked.

'My aunt,' he said sadly. 'Or rather, my great-aunt – she's my grandfather's sister.'

'And why were you following her?'

He sighed, reluctant to speak for a moment. 'I think she's turned to a life of crime. I think she's been stealing credit cards.'

CHAPTER
TWO

'AND WHAT MAKES YOU SAY THAT?' I asked.

'A few days ago,' said Skull, 'I was clearing my homework off the dining room table, and I accidentally knocked Great Aunt Mirna's handbag off the chair she'd left it on. All her stuff spilled out across the floor. I was embarrassed, but there was nobody else around so I quickly gathered everything up and put it back in the handbag.'

'But not before you'd noticed something odd?' I suggested.

'Right,' replied Skull. 'There were several credit cards in among everything else. I'm pretty sure Aunt Mirna doesn't even have a bank account, not in this country, let alone any credit cards. Besides, each card had a different name on it.'

'What names? Anyone you know?' I asked.

He thought for a moment. 'Umm, I think one of them might have been . . . er, Robinson? I don't know, I can't remember.'

Great. No help at all. Thanks. 'No problem,' I said with a smile.

'I was just worried about getting everything back in the bag, so nobody would notice,' explained Skull.

'But you're sure that's what you saw?' I said. 'You couldn't have been mistaken?'

'Yes and no. I mean, yes I'm sure, no I wasn't mistaken.'

I huddled up in my blanket. It felt like the temperature in the shed was falling faster than a giant rock chucked off a cliff. I decided to gather the facts as quickly as possible.

'Why would Aunt Mirna turn to crime?' I asked.

'Well, she has no money,' said Skull, shrugging. 'She's got quite a bit coming, but it hasn't turned up yet.'

'Why is that? You said she didn't have a bank account in this country? She's been living abroad?'

'Oh no, she'd never even been to the UK until nearly three months ago,' said Skull. 'She's lived in Vojvladimia all her life.'

'Veggie-where?' I muttered.

11

'Voj-vlad-eee-me-a,' repeated Skull slowly.

I think I must have stared blankly at him. Either that or the cold had frozen my face.

'In the Balkans?' Skull went on. 'Where my family comes from? Remember?'

I suddenly remembered. 'Oh yeah! Sorry!' I cried, going a bit red.

What I'd remembered was that Skull had stood up in class a couple of terms ago and told us about his family tree. We were doing a history project on ancestors. For most of the class, research had turned up nothing terribly interesting, but not in Peter Skulyevic's case.

For generations, the Skulyevic family had lived in the tiny Balkan province of Vojvladimia. (I had no idea where that was. I hadn't wanted to say I had no idea where that was, so I had quietly looked it up when I got home – according to my atlas, it's a little crinkly rectangle on the coast of the Adriatic Sea, just opposite Italy. I really ought to pay more attention during geography.)

About thirty-something years ago, there was a civil war in Vojvladimia and the government was taken over by the army. The guy in charge was a brutal dictator who started locking up anyone he didn't like. And if he *really* didn't like them, he had them shot. Among the many, many people he disliked was Emerik Skulyevic, Peter's granddad. Emerik was quite a well-known poet, and had been very critical of the army.

Emerik managed to escape along with his seven-year-old son Antonin, Peter's dad, by hiding in the back of a truck that was leaving the country. On the way, the truck drove through a military camp filled with soldiers who would have killed the pair of them on sight if they'd been caught.

Emerik and young Antonin arrived as refugees in the UK a few months later. From that point on, Emerik campaigned against the dictator and also continued to be quite a well-known poet. Five years ago, the military government in Vojvladimia was finally overthrown. Freedom returned and everyone who'd been locked up was released.

Peter's granddad intended to return to his homeland at once, but he needed a hip operation and couldn't travel until he was fully recovered. Sadly, he died before he could make the trip and see Vojvladimia again.

As Peter had finished his story, standing at the front of the classroom, there was absolute silence. Mrs Penzler, our form tutor, had dabbed her eyes with a tissue.

'Did he not make it through the operation, Peter?' she'd asked softly.

'Yes, but he got run over by an ambulance on the way out of the hospital,' Peter had told us. 'Sad, really. His new hip was so good he was walking faster than he'd done in years.'

'Oh,' Mrs Penzler had said. She'd turned to the class. 'Any questions?'

Almost everyone had put up their hand. The girls had wanted to hear some of Emerik's poetry. The boys had wanted to know how many people the army had shot.

Meanwhile, back in my freezing cold shed, Skull continued.

'After Vojvladimia was freed, my dad often wondered what had become of Granddad's sister, Mirna. Dad really didn't remember her, it was too long ago, but she would have been the only other member of the Skulyevic family still alive. She'd been arrested by the army before Emerik could escape. Throughout the dictatorship there was very little information allowed in or out of the country, and Emerik never heard from her again. So you can imagine how overjoyed Dad was when she called us, out of the blue, a few months ago.'

'I have to ask this,' I said. 'You're sure it was really her?'

Skull nodded. 'We all asked exactly the same thing. But there's no doubt. She's got her passport, and various odds and ends from years ago, and she definitely recognised Dad from when he was a boy. Mirna is definitely Mirna. She's, er, what's the phrase . . . quite a character.'

'Which is what adults say when they mean "a right

pain in the backside",' I translated.

Skull pulled a kind of yeah-hmm-oh-well face. 'She's loads of fun, always making us laugh. But she's a bit . . . dippy. She found some varnish in the cupboard under the stairs and painted the kitchen walls with it. And she keeps phoning all the neighbours and having street parties at eleven o'clock at night. Dad says we've all got to remember that she spent years locked up by the military. She's bound to be a bit eccentric.'

'And she lives with you now?' I said.

Yeah-hmm-oh-well-face. 'When she turned up in person, nine weeks ago, she said she was staying for a few days and would be off on her travels again. She's decided to see the world, you see, enjoy her freedom after being imprisoned for so long.'

'Good for her. But . . . ?'

'But she's still sleeping in the spare room. She got to the UK by doing odd jobs and spending her earnings on train tickets. But she's got no money at all at the moment. She's waiting for some bank in Vojvladimia to forward her a load of cash it's been holding. I don't quite understand the details of it. There's some sort of mix-up.'

'Could she borrow some money?'

'Mum and Dad have offered to lend her some, but she won't take it. Which is kind of a relief, because we haven't got any spare anyway. She keeps saying she

15

wants to send us on holiday as soon as her money comes through. A few weeks ago, Dad happened to mention that we hadn't been able to afford our usual week at the seaside for a couple of years, so Mirna's insisting she pay. She says we're her only family, and she wants to repay us for welcoming her and letting her stay and all that.'

'What do your mum and dad think about that?' I asked.

'To be perfectly honest,' sighed Skull, 'Mum's counting the minutes till the money arrives and Mirna can be off on her travels again. Dad thinks much the same, but he won't say so. As far as he's concerned, she's his last relative, his last link back to Vojvladimia, so although she's a bit of a handful, he likes having her around. I mean, we're all very fond of her, it's just that . . .'

'She's a bit of a handful,' I said. 'And now there's this business with the credit cards.'

'Exactly,' said Skull. He shifted forward in the chair. In the shed's icy chill, our breath puffed like balls of steam. 'I'm really worried she's getting into trouble. I think she's stealing because she's got no money. I think all those years locked up have taken their toll on her.'

'Do you have any other leads to follow?' I asked. 'When you followed her earlier today, where did she go?'

'I've kept a close eye on her for days,' said Skull. 'But she's done nothing suspicious. This morning, she said she was going to visit this lady she's got friendly with from the Post Office who lives in Doyle Avenue. And that's what she did! Straight to number eighteen, stayed for forty-five minutes and straight home again. Then I came here to see you.'

'You can stop worrying,' I declared, 'Saxby Smart is on the case! I think the first thing for me to do is to meet Great Aunt Mirna myself. I'll come over to your house after school tomorrow.'

'Thanks,' said Skull with a smile. Well, a broader smile than the one he always had.

I put my case notes away in my filing cabinet and we made our way out of the shed. Skull paused at the garden gate which leads on to the alleyway behind the houses.

'By the way,' he said, 'if Mirna *has* turned to a life of crime, if she *has* been stealing credit cards . . . you won't tell the police, will you? I mean, I just want her to stop. You know, see the error of her ways. We'd all be horrified if she ended up being arrested in this country, too! Especially Dad.'

At first, I wasn't sure what to say. In the end, what I did say was: 'You mean, you want me to turn a blind eye if she's guilty?'

'Yes.'

What? *What?*

'Er, I see,' I muttered. 'Let's, um, let's hope she's innocent . . .'

17

A Page From My Notebook

OK, let's review the basic facts.

1. Great Aunt Mirna has very little money.
2. Great Aunt Mirna has credit cards in her purse.
3. The credit cards are not in Great Aunt Mirna's name.
Conclusion: Great Aunt Mirna has nicked the credit cards. This looks like an open-and-shut case!

BUT IS IT? Could there be an innocent explanation? What other explanations might there be . . .?
1. Mirna is looking after the cards for a friend. This seems unlikely. Why would she? And for half a dozen friends?
2. Mirna has applied for credit cards using fake names. That's a huge no-no in itself! That's called fraud!
3. Mirna just happened to find these cards lying in the street. Also unlikely. Why hasn't she said anything? Why is she keeping them?
4. Mirna has a new hobby – making imitation credit cards out of salt dough and cardboard. Kind of a handicraft. Yeah, right.

So! COULD there be an innocent explanation? Doesn't look like it . . .

WAIT! HUGE moral dilemma!

ON THE ONE HAND: If Mirna is guilty, then I have a duty to say so. If I turn a blind eye, I wouldn't simply be bending the rules, I'd be tying them in a knot. What about the people whose credit cards have been stolen? If one of them came to me for help, I wouldn't hesitate to expose whoever was guilty. Justice must apply to EVERYONE, EQUALLY. What right do I have to make an exception?

ON THE OTHER HAND: Mirna has had a tough life and she's poor and she's finally made contact with her family again. If she's guilty, couldn't things be put right quietly and Mirna's crime be looked on as a one-off, a bad mistake? Should I take her circumstances into account? SHOULD I show more compassion?

Can ANY crime be excused? Or justified? If so, to what extent? If not, why? If Mirna IS guilty and I tell the world, then whose side would I be on? Whose side SHOULD I be on?

Perhaps . . . I should turn the job down? No, that would be chickening out. And I don't do that.

Perhaps . . . I should do what I've always told myself a good detective should do – remain OBJECTIVE and IMPARTIAL and DETACHED.

I really, really, REALLY hope she's innocent . . .

CHAPTER THREE

THE FOLLOWING AFTERNOON, MONDAY, Skull and I walked back to his house after school. Although his street was only a short walk from my own, the houses were very different. They were sort of boxish and arranged in pairs, two separate homes forming one chunky building. They had tall roofs and regularly-spaced windows, which made them look rather toy-like, as if some giant kid had clicked them all together to make a play road.

Skull's house was towards the far end of the street. Unlike most of the neighbouring houses, his had a small porch built on to the front. There was also a garage attached to the side, which I guessed was a fairly recent addition. Its shallow-sloped roof made it look like that giant kid had been in a hurry and left it leaning against the main bulk of the house.

Skull's dad was cooking the tea, his mum was still at her desk in the dining room. (Both Skull's parents worked from home, after having been made redundant from other jobs the previous year.) Great Aunt Mirna was sitting in the living room, flicking through a hefty catalogue from a DIY store.

'Sledgehammers . . . sledgehammers . . .' she muttered to herself as she whipped pages aside. 'Chain saws, no . . . Cement mixers, no . . .'

'What do you want a sledgehammer for?' said Skull.

Mirna grinned up at him. She had a round, wrinkly face with owlish glasses. Her dark hair, silver at the roots where she hadn't dyed it for a while, was pinned up in a bun. 'Your father's going to get rid of this hideous fireplace,' she said brightly. Her East European accent was very broad, but her English was excellent. 'This room always did look better without it. Nobody around here has one of these hideous things in their lounge any more!'

She was right, the fireplace was indeed hideous. It was one of those thick, lumpy stone things you see in places which haven't been redecorated since about 1985. It was a total fake as well – the house had no chimney, the wall where the fireplace stood backed on to the garage!

'Aunt Mirna,' protested Skull, 'Dad built that fireplace

himself. I'm sure he's never even mentioned it to you, let alone said he wanted it gone.'

Mirna frowned to herself, letting the catalogue on her knees close with a slap. 'Well, he definitely said he wanted *something* gone,' she said.

Skull shot me a let's-change-the-subject look. 'This is my friend Saxby,' he said.

'Hello,' said Aunt Mirna, giving me a firm handshake. 'Nice to meet you, Saxby. That's a very unusual name.'

'It's medieval, apparently,' I said with a smile. 'I've been hearing all about the Skulyevic family history. I expect it's wonderful to have found Skull, er, I mean, Peter here and his mum and dad after all this time.'

Mirna sat back in her armchair with a soppy expression on her face. Her spindly hands grasped one of Skull's, and she patted it gently as she spoke.

'Thoughts of my family are what kept me going,' she said, 'through the dark years of military rule in my country. In a strange way, I suffered much less than a lot of people in Vojvladimia. I wasn't mistreated in that prison and at least I was fed. Plenty can't even say that. My only regret is that I'm here too late to see my brother Emerik again. I did miss him, all those years. But at least we still have his work, we have his poetry.'

'Yes,' said Skull. He turned to me. 'Have you read any of my granddad's poems?'

'Actually, no. But I'd like to,' I said. To be perfectly honest, I was only being polite. I've never been much of a poetry fan. There are a couple of limericks I like, but that's my limit, really.

Skull and Great Aunt Mirna bustled over to the bookshelves and started taking down armfuls of slightly faded little hardbacks. As I watched them, reluctantly I had to marvel at Mirna. She had obviously settled into the Skulyevic household as comfortably as if she really was one of the family.

She *might* have been Mirna Skulyevic. But I was having doubts. She *might* have been telling the truth about her past. But I had reason to believe that there was something sinister going on here. Something that went way beyond any stolen credit cards.

Have you spotted why I was suspicious? There was a mismatch between what 'Mirna' had said, and what Skull had told me back in the shed. She *might* have made a simple slip of the tongue, but her English was otherwise perfect. I was on my guard.

Can you work out what was troubling me?

The day before, Skull had told me that Mirna had never left Vojvladimia until a few weeks ago. OK. So, why did she say, referring to the hideous fireplace, 'This room always did look better without it'?

When exactly could she possibly have seen this room before? She'd been out of touch with the family for years, she can't even have seen photos or been told about it.

As I said just now, it *might* have been a slip of the tongue, but it seemed unlikely when her command of English was so good. Besides, she also said that 'Nobody around here has one of these hideous things in their lounge any more'. An odd thing to know, if you've never even visited the country before. Besides, she also said 'That's a very unusual name'. I suppose if she'd studied English, she'd have an idea of what sort of names were common or not in the UK, but on top of everything else, I couldn't help feeling it was a suspiciously precise thing to say.

Skull handed me one of the books they'd gathered up. It was a slim, slightly dusty volume, a bit dog-eared at the corners. While Skull and Mirna eyed me eagerly, I opened the book at random and read aloud the first poem that caught my eye. It began:

BEAUTY
O swiftly, swiftly, swiftly,
Falls the jam, plopping like a sandwich
There
Upon the carpet, upon the dancing mice
That spin eternal webs of sorrow
O'er frog, and tree, and bicycle . . .

I had to stop there. I'm no judge of good poetry but I was pretty sure I'd never heard such a load of old rubbish in all my life. Maybe it lost something in translation into English. Or maybe not.

'Beautiful,' muttered Mirna. 'Emerik had such a lyrical turn of phrase.'

'It's good, isn't it?' said Skull. 'My granddad's still Vojvladimia's greatest-ever poet.'

Good grief.

'Emerik's poems are so powerfully rich in symbols and meaning,' said Mirna, her eyes shining with pride.

'Yes,' I said, 'they're very, er . . . moving.'

Fortunately, tea was ready at that exact moment, so we all went to eat. Unfortunately, Mirna and Skull kept reading out sections of Emerik Skulyevic's poetry all through the meal. Soon, Skull's mum and dad were joining in and reciting stuff from memory. There was a weird little verse about zebras and an even weirder little

25

verse about telephones made out of cheese, or something like that. I was trying not to listen – it nearly put me off my food.

A little while later, as I was zipping up my coat and pulling on my woolly hat before heading home in the freezing cold, I managed to have a quiet word with Skull in the narrow hallway which led to the front door.

'Whatever you do,' I whispered, 'don't take any further action. You don't need to keep tabs on what Mirna is up to or anything like that.'

I was careful to make sure I said nothing about my suspicions. I needed to establish the truth before making any accusations. If I was right, it was vitally important that Skull did nothing to alert Mirna to the possibility that her cover was blown.

'You think she's innocent, then?' hissed Skull hopefully.

'I think it's absolutely essential that you do nothing,' I whispered. 'Leave it to me. Understood?'

'Aye, aye,' whispered Skull, doing a miniature salute.

The doorbell rang. It turned out to be a delivery man from SuperSave, with a week's worth of groceries.

'My parents get everything online,' tutted Skull, as the delivery man hefted boxes into the kitchen. 'They don't go anywhere from one week to the next. Too busy working. I swear they'd never leave the house if they had the choice. Oh, by the way, before you go, I thought you might like to borrow this.'

He handed me the volume of Emerik Skulyevic's poetry we'd been looking at before tea. 'You seemed so keen on my granddad's work, I thought you might like to read more of it.'

'That's . . . very kind of you,' I said weakly, as I took it from him. 'I'll, um, look forward to it.'

When I got home, I phoned my great friend Isobel 'Izzy' Moustique, St Egbert's School's top brainiac and all-round Information Guru. I told her all about the Skulyevic situation and asked her to dig up whatever research might be relevant.

After that, I went and huddled up in my Thinking Chair, wrapped in the chunkiest blanket I could find. It seemed that there was much more to this case than there'd first appeared. Whatever was going on, it went way beyond a few stolen credit cards.

A Page From My Notebook

Whichever way I approach this problem, it gets more tangled-up and mind-baffling the more I think about it!

Could I have got things the wrong way around? COULD Mirna actually BE Mirna? If not, WHO IS SHE? If so, where am I going wrong?

Could it be that I've allowed myself to get sidetracked? Could SOMEONE ELSE be the guilty party? Could someone else have PLANTED those credit cards on Mirna, knowing that she's a little absent-minded?

No, wait a minute. That creates even MORE questions:

1. WHY would someone else be doing it?

2. WHO might this someone else be?

• Surely not Skull himself – he alerted me to the problem! Or might that be a double bluff?

• Could it be Skull's MUM? Could it be Skull's dad, ANTONIN? Mirna appears to have outstayed her welcome, with Skull's mum at least. BUT . . .to deliberately implicate Mirna in a crime? That's a bit drastic, surely?

All in all, I think the most likely scenario is still that Mirna is a phoney. BUT . . . if so, how do we explain the passport, other documents and personal odds and ends Skull says she's got?

Is Mirna innocent? Is she as guilty as a toddler with chocolate all round its mouth? If she's the phoney I suspect, I'm left with a problem: Have I got the heart to reveal to the Skulyevic family that she's a total fake?

CHAPTER
FOUR

SS-PLOPP! A QUIVERING DOLLOP OF what looked like scrambled egg landed on my plate.

'Sorry,' I said to the rock-faced dinner lady, giving her my nicest smile. 'Um, I asked for the vegetable pie?'

The rock-faced dinner lady glared at me. 'That *is* the vegetable pie,' she grumbled.

'Thanks very much, looks delicious,' I said quickly. I hurried away from the lunch queue and found somewhere to sit.

It was the day following my visit to Skull's house, and as Skull and I were in different groups for most subjects, I hadn't yet seen him to make sure he was doing as he was told – leaving the whole Mirna situation well alone.

As I was beginning to prod the vegetable pie with a fork and worrying that it might start prodding me back, I was joined by Izzy. We swapped notes for a couple of minutes about how aaaawwwful the history supply teacher was. Izzy flipped open her sandwich box and started nibbling at an exotic-looking wholemeal wrap filled with interesting sauces.

'That looks nice,' I said, hungrily.

'It is,' she said.

'Got a spare one?'

'No.'

I went back to prodding the pie. 'Did you find out anything after I called last night?'

'Yes, I certainly did!' declared Izzy. She dusted crumbs from her fingers and pulled a folder from her school bag. 'Although I have a feeling you may already know most of it.'

'Never mind, let's hear what you've got,' I said, chancing a sniff at the pie. Smelled OK, actually.

Izzy flipped a few sheets out of the folder. 'You've heard of the Minkstreet and Batt bullion robbery?'

If I'd dared to start eating any of that pie, I'd now have spluttered it back out again. 'You bet I have!' I cried. 'Third biggest robbery of gold bars in English criminal history! A bunch of crooks got away with about thirty million pounds' worth, if I remember right?'

Izzy consulted her print-outs. 'Thirty-two and a half million,' she said, nodding. 'The Minkstreet and Batt Investment Bank was reckoned to have the most secure underground vault in London. The thieves burned their way through the door.'

'That's going back a while, isn't it?' I said. 'Wasn't it about forty years ago?'

Izzy consulted her print-outs again. 'Forty-one,' she said.

I screwed up my face trying to recall the details of the case. (Note to self: one day, put together a proper encyclopedia-type book on all these old real-life investigations! Sherlock Holmes kept saying he'd do it, and he never did! Don't make the same mistake!)

'They were all caught,' I said. 'It took several weeks, and the gang had split up the gold and gone their separate ways, but they were all tracked down in the end. What was the name of the leader? She was a *really* nasty piece of work.'

Izzy read from her notes. 'Elsa Moreaux. Half French, half German. You're right, she had a long list of convictions for various violent armed robberies, starting from when she was just nineteen. Once she was locked up, she quickly got a reputation as the prison's toughest and most intimidating inmate.'

Izzy slipped a sheet of paper over to me. Among all

the data was a photo of Elsa Moreaux, taken in a police station. It showed a young woman with fair hair, holding up a prisoner number and scowling at the camera in a way which would make even a rock-faced dinner lady dive for cover.

'That's the only known picture of her,' said Izzy, 'taken thirty-eight years ago. According to several sources, she was unchained for two minutes while they took that shot, and in that time she managed to knock out four guards and badly injure another three. And break the camera. Very dangerous lady.'

'She looks it,' I whistled. 'Am I right in thinking they never recovered her share of the gold? Worth about seven or eight million pounds?'

'Correct,' said Izzy. 'All the rest was traced, but hers has never been found.'

'Must be worth several million more in today's money,' I muttered to myself.

'Now then,' said Izzy, leaning over the table. 'I've dug up a couple of facts about her you may *not* know.' For a moment, I thought she was about to do her slightly smug eyebrow-raising thing (which always happens when she thinks she's proving she's cleverer than I am! Huh!) But she didn't. This was obviously serious stuff she'd discovered.

'Fact number one,' she continued, 'Elsa Moreaux

was finally released from prison just over a year ago. The police kept a twenty-four hour watch on her from that moment on.'

'Why? Because of the missing gold?'

'Exactly. She must have got fed up of all the surveillance though, because she left the country nine months ago and hasn't come back.'

'Are the police sure about that?' I asked.

'All airports, rail terminals and coastal authorities have had her on their Top Priority lists ever since,' said Izzy. 'Not a sign of her. The cops currently think she's in Spain, running a sushi bar.'

I scratched my chin in a very detectivey way. 'This is all very well,' I said, 'but what's it got to do with the Skulyevic situation?'

'Ah, that's where we come to fact number two,' said Izzy. 'I'll give you one guess what Elsa Moreaux's home address was in the years before she got caught for the Minkstreet and Batt job.'

It's not often I can honestly say that a cold shiver went down my spine. But a cold shiver did exactly that, right there and then.

'Skull's house?'

I gasped. Izzy nodded slowly.

'But that means . . .!' I gasped.

Izzy nodded slowly.

This information suddenly opened up a couple of obvious possibilities about Mirna.

I'm sure you've already spotted them both.

Possibility 1: If Mirna *was* a phoney, could she actually be Elsa Moreaux?

Possibility 2: If so, could it be that she had returned to her old house to reclaim the gold bullion she'd stolen forty years ago?

'No,' said Izzy. 'I can see what you're thinking, Saxby, and I'm afraid the answer is no. Her old house – Skull's current address – is the one place the police are sure she *didn't* hide the gold. After she was arrested, they searched every last millimetre of the house. They took out the kitchen cupboards, they lifted all the floorboards, they ripped all the furniture apart, they stripped the whole place bare. They dug up the entire garden, too, down to a depth of five metres. Here, take a look at this.'

She passed me another print-out. It was a clipping from a newspaper dated shortly after Elsa Moreaux's arrest. A photo showed Skull's house as it had been forty years before, without its porch or garage and with climbing roses growing up a tall trellis beside the front door.

'Hmm,' I muttered to myself, 'at least I was right about that garage being built recently.'

The photo also showed various uniformed police officers milling about outside the house. Beside them was a huge pile of wrecked furniture. Beside the pile was an enormous mechanical digger, and behind the digger was a series of earth mounds where the garden had once been.

'They almost literally took the place apart,' said Izzy. 'No gold. Wherever Elsa Moreaux is, the secret of where it's hidden is lost along with her. And, don't forget, she's out of the UK. The authorities are still watching out for her.'

I sighed. Then I sighed again. I had to agree with Izzy – it looked like I'd been jumping to conclusions.

If the stolen gold wasn't hidden in Elsa Moreaux's old house, what possible reason could she have for returning there?

What reason could I have to think that Elsa Moreaux had come back to the UK anyway? I had no reason to doubt that she really was in . . . Where was it, Spain?

'Spain, yes,' said Izzy. 'I have a feeling that maybe the Elsa Moreaux connection is just a coincidence. There's a mystery to be solved here – the mystery surrounding those credit cards – and perhaps the fact that Skull's house has an interesting story attached to it has sidetracked us?'

'Yes, could be,' I mumbled. However, I was still troubled by the idea that Mirna was a fake. If she wasn't the notorious Elsa Moreaux, she was still *somebody*.

'Talking of credit cards,' I said, 'did you find anything out on that score?'

'Sorry, nothing at all,' said Izzy. 'There's no way I can access records on that sort of thing. I've got no way of checking up on a stolen card. In any case, credit card theft is quite common. Even if I could track down records of stolen cards, working out which ones Mirna might have nicked would be like finding a needle in a load of haystacks. Sorry.'

'No problem,' I sighed. 'Thanks anyway.'

Izzy finished off her wrap and neatly pierced her carton of apple juice with its little plastic straw. 'On the other hand, there's an absolute lorry-load of info about Emerik Skulyevic available. Articles, reviews, all sorts. There were a lot of interviews with him published after the dictatorship in Vojvladimia was overthrown, stuff about his work, his family, his life. Have you read any of Emerik Skulyevic's poetry?'

I shuddered slightly. 'Have you?'

'Yes,' said Izzy. 'He's reckoned to have had a very lyrical turn of phrase and to have written poems powerfully rich in symbols and meaning.'

'Really?'

'Yes. But I thought it was a load of old rubbish, personally.'

'Fair enough,' I said. 'It's a pity we don't know anyone who actually lives in Vojvladimia right now. This whole problem is made even harder to sort out by the fact that Mirna's turned up out of the blue.'

'I could ask around on my FaceSpace page,' said Izzy, clipping the lid back on her lunchbox. 'Someone might know someone who might know someone.'

'Good idea, keep digging,' I said.

Izzy gave me a nod and headed off back to class. I took a last jab at the vegetable pie. Tasted OK, after all.

The one thought that went through my head at that moment was: Thank goodness I told Skull to take no further action. If Mirna really *does* turn out to be a dangerous criminal on the scale of Elsa Moreaux, there could be a *terrible* risk in doing anything which might alert her to my investigation. It was even more vital that Skull kept silent about our suspicions.

A school bag clunked down on to the table next to me. I looked up to find Skull beaming away.

'Hey, guess what?' he said, pointing to the bag. 'I've swiped Great Aunt Mirna's box of treasures, complete with her passport and everything. We could search it all for clues. She probably won't know it's gone. Not until about five o'clock, anyway.'

I slapped a hand to my face.

CHAPTER FIVE

I WAS TOO FURIOUS WITH SKULL to do or say anything straight away. I managed to growl a few words, such as 'twit', 'idiot' and 'never listen to a bloomin' word I say', before the bell went for the start of afternoon lessons.

By the time the bell went at the end of afternoon lessons, I'd calmed down a bit. As a steady flow of pupils bubbled up and down the school corridors, I grabbed Skull and we walked through the cloakroom and out of the main building.

'Right, we'd better make the best of a bad job,' I said, zipping up my coat. 'Let's see what you've got.'

'Sorry,' muttered Skull, 'I just wanted to clear Mirna's name as quickly as possible.'

'Yeah, yeah, yeah,' I grumbled. 'What's in the bag?'

Inside Skull's school bag was a rectangular wooden box, about the size of a large cake tin. It was covered in delicately carved patterns.

'My dad remembers this box from when he was very little,' said Skull, 'from before Granddad Emerik fled Vojvladimia. It's been in the family for two centuries.'

'It's beautiful,' I said.

Skull opened it up. The inside of the box was crammed with all kinds of papers, old photographs and odds and ends. There was a small puppet-like toy, also wooden, held together at the joints with tiny twists of wire.

'Granddad Emerik made that for my dad on the day he was born. When Dad saw that again he almost cried!'

There were a selection of official documents written in Vojvlic (the version of the Croatian language used in Vojvladimia), including what looked like a couple of birth certificates. There was a picture, faded and crumpled, showing a tall man standing in a doorway, wearing a baggy suit.

'That's Granddad Emerik,' said Skull. 'That was taken on the day his first book of poetry was published. Look, he's put a date and his signature on the back.'

He had indeed. Out of the box I also took a glossy, freshly issued passport. In it were Mirna Skulyevic's photo and details, plus a series of border stamps

41

showing that she'd left Vojvladimia, travelled across Europe and arrived in the UK in exactly the way she'd described to Skull's family.

'Well?' said Skull. 'What do you think?'

There was only one thing I *could* think. It was impossible, quite impossible, that all these things could have been faked or happened upon by chance. Clearly, much of it was verifiable as genuine by Skull's dad, Antonin.

There was only one conclusion I could come to, a conclusion which finally cleared up the question of Mirna's true identity. I could now be sure of one absolutely definite fact.

Can you see what that fact was?

Mirna *was* Mirna. The Mirna Skulyevic living at Skull's house was the genuine article. She really was his great-aunt. Nobody else could be in possession of all this stuff.

All that information about the infamous Elsa Moreaux *was* just a distraction. Izzy had been correct. The link between Skull's house and that bank robbery from forty-odd years ago was nothing more than a coincidence.

(Which was good news. I didn't like the thought of coming face to face with someone as violently dangerous as Elsa Moreaux!)

'Skull, I've changed my mind,' I declared. 'You bringing me all this stuff has been very helpful.'

'Really?'

'Really. It's allowed me to focus my investigation.' We were nearing the school gates. Kids were dispersing across the playground and the road beyond. 'Now, hurry up and get that box back, before it's missed!'

'Right away!' said Skull.

He trotted off ahead of me. I was left feeling extremely pleased that some of the dense mist surrounding this case had finally started to clear.

However . . .

There was still the important matter of the credit cards to sort out. And the matter of the strange things Mirna had said when I'd visited Skull's house – the strange things she'd said which had led me to doubt her identity in the first place.

I drifted into thought. I also drifted slap bang into my other great friend George 'Muddy' Whitehouse, the school's leading expert in all things gadget-related. I nearly knocked him off his feet.

'Sorry, Muddy! I was busy thinking!'

'Haven't seen you for a couple of days, Saxby,' he said cheerily. As usual, he was looking like a walking rubbish tip, littered with assorted mud, oil and food stains. He scratched at a yellow one on his pullover. I think it was the vegetable pie from lunchtime. 'You on an investigation?' he asked.

'Yes, I'm in the middle of a very puzzling problem,' I said.

'*The Case of the Doyle Avenue Forger*, is it?' he said.

'Huh?' I blinked. 'I don't know what you're talking about.'

'It was on the news this morning. Didn't you see it? The police raided a flat opposite where whassisname in Mr Prunely's class lives.'

'No,' I shrugged. 'What was going on?'

'The bloke who lived there got dragged out kicking and screaming in the early hours, apparently. He had a flat full of fake documents – forged banknotes, certificates, passports, money-off coupons, plastic parking permits, lottery tickets – everything you could think of. They've been after him for years. He had a whole forgery factory in there. Whassisname was telling me all about it.'

Suddenly, I stopped dead.

Those dense mists I mentioned, surrounding this case? They were clearing faster than ever!

I'd solved the mystery of the credit cards. They weren't stolen at all, they were forgeries, made by this guy who'd just been caught.

How did I know? Think way back, to something Skull told me when he visited my garden shed.

Can you spot the connection between Mirna and the forger?

'This flat in Doyle Avenue,' I said urgently, 'was it number eighteen?'

'Er, yes, I think whassisname did say eighteen, yes,' replied Muddy. 'I thought you said you hadn't seen the news?'

'I didn't,' I said. 'The day he came to see me, Skull followed Mirna to number eighteen Doyle Avenue. She wasn't visiting a "friend from the Post Office" though, she was getting hold of forged credit cards.'

'Now I don't know what *you're* talking about,' said Muddy.

'*Can* you forge credit cards?' I asked. 'I thought that sort of thing was very difficult these days, what with all the chips and other security in them?'

'Oh yeah, it's difficult,' said Muddy, 'but not impossible. This guy they just caught must have been using some cutting-edge tech. My guess – from an electronics point of view – is that each card would only have been of use once or twice before it was detected.'

'Which explains why Mirna had half a dozen in her bag,' I said. 'She's probably been getting through heaps of them. And now her supply has been turned off!'

I thanked Muddy and zoomed out of the school gates. All the way home, fresh questions and ideas kept popping into my brain like lightbulbs being switched on.

I definitely *was* going to have to reveal Mirna's

activities to the rest of the Skulyevic family. However, I would still need to handle the matter delicately. What I had to establish now was what Mirna had been using those forged credit cards *for*. That was now the key to the whole thing. Once I could work out *how* Mirna had been using the cards, I would have the complete picture.

As to her *motive*, the reason she'd done it, well . . . Skull had said she had very little cash. Perhaps she'd got fed up of waiting for her money to be transferred from Vojvladimia? Perhaps those years of being locked up by the military government had affected her more than anyone thought? Perhaps her new-found freedom had gone to her head and she'd taken things too far?

Another coincidental link between Mirna and Elsa Moreaux – a sad one this time – suddenly occurred to me. They'd both spent decades in prison, but it was the one who'd been innocent for all those years who was now guilty of a crime and who'd probably end up going back behind bars.

This was one case I really wasn't looking forward to wrapping up. It felt as if everyone involved, me included, would be losing out in one way or another.

An hour or two later, I got a call from Izzy.

'Anything turned up?' I said.

'Yes,' said Izzy. 'But you're not going to like it.'

47

'I'm feeling that way already,' I told her.

'I had a search around through FaceSpace and one of my cousins has some FaceSpace friends in various parts of Eastern Europe —'

(Not surprising. Izzy had nineteen cousins at the last count, and they were all just like her. I'd have been surprised if one of them *hadn't* known anyone in Eastern Europe! For more info on Izzy's vast family connections, see volume four of my case files, *The Hangman's Lair*.)

'— and I've found out something very important about Mirna Skulyevic.'

'Yes?'

'You're really not going to like it,' said Izzy.

'Just tell me.'

'You're sure?'

'Yes!'

'OK. Mirna Skulyevic . . .'

'Yes?'

'The real Mirna Skulyevic, the sister of Emerik Skulyevic . . .'

'Yeeeees! What?'

' . . . died in Vojvladimia nearly seventeen years ago.'

I froze in horror. The phone dropped from my fingers and clattered to the floor.

CHAPTER
SIX

B-B-But . . .! WHAT? . . . HOW? . . . WHEN? . . . WHY? . . .
Huh?

The mind-boggling consequences of what Izzy had just told me were boggling my mind more than it had ever been boggled before. And, what with one thing and another, my mind's been boggled *a lot*!

After a couple of minutes, I regained the power of speech. I scooped up the phone and said, in a feeble voice, 'Are you sure?'

'Totally,' said Izzy. 'Why is that such a shock? You told me the woman at Skull's house wasn't Mirna anyway.'

'Yes . . . but . . . er . . . but . . . this afternoon, I saw conclusive proof that she *is* Mirna Skulyevic.'

'That's not possible. She's dead. I mean, unless Skull's

got a zombie or something living with him, that woman is an imposter.'

I held a hand to my forehead, as if I was trying to stop my mind from overflowing. 'Wait a minute. How can Mirna have died years ago and Skull's family be unaware of that?'

'The country was under a ruthless military dictatorship until very recently, remember,' Izzy reminded me. 'Mirna was locked away by the government. Very few people *over there* knew she'd died, let alone anyone *over here*!'

'OK, OK,' I said, trying to get my head around it all. 'How do you know this? What exactly have you discovered?'

'Well,' said Izzy, 'basically, one of my cousin's FaceSpace friends knows people in the area of Vojvladimia where the Skulyevic family comes from. Many people there knew Emerik at least, because he was such a well-known poet. Several people who knew Mirna personally swear she died years ago. One of them, a close friend of hers, was given all her belongings because there were no more members of the family in the country at the time.'

'Belongings?' I said. That wooden box Skull had shown me!

'There were various bits and pieces,' said Izzy. 'I don't

know the exact details. They were all packed into one carved wooden box. Some sort of family heirloom, apparently.'

My heart nearly skipped a beat. 'What happened to the box?'

'It was given to an English researcher who was in Vojvladimia a few months ago,' said Izzy.

'Researcher? Researching what?'

'Emerik Skulyevic. An English woman visited the area, gathering any information she could about him and his life. She's writing his biography, his life story. She's going to establish an Emerik Skulyevic permanent exhibition in one of the London museums.'

By now, my heart was skipping along to whatever beat it happened to fancy. 'What was her name?'

'Janet Smith. Which isn't helpful. There must be hundreds of Janet Smiths around!'

'Yes, quite.' I smiled to myself.

'I've tried to find out if this biography she's working on is due out soon,' said Izzy, 'but no luck. None of the online bookshops have it listed.'

'They wouldn't have,' I said. 'I think the whole biography thing is a lie.'

'Are you sure?'

'Not quite. I will be in a few minutes. See you at school tomorrow.'

I sent a text to Skull: *Quick question – has your dad heard of anyone called Janet Smith? Has he been contacted by anyone writing a biography of Emerik Skulyevic?*

The reply was: *No, and no. Why?*

I was right. Whoever Janet Smith was, she certainly wasn't writing Emerik's biography. For one very simple reason.

Have you spotted it too?

Surely, nobody who was writing someone's life story would fail to talk to that person's son? Any brief glance at the available info on Emerik Skulyevic would reveal that Emerik had a son, Antonin – Skull's dad.

As soon as Izzy had mentioned this Janet Smith, I wondered why Skull's family – being so proud of Emerik – hadn't mentioned this biography to me. The reason was they'd never heard of it, or of Janet Smith. Conclusion: 'Janet Smith' wasn't really doing this research at all!

(Of course, it *could* have been that she was real and *was* researching a biography, but was simply a complete twit for not knowing about and/or not contacting Antonin. However, since I'd already established that something dodgy was going on, this didn't exactly seem likely.)

For a minute or two, I felt extremely pleased with myself, because I'd so quickly realised that this mysterious 'researcher' was nothing of the kind. But then . . .

Several increasingly uncomfortable thoughts occurred to me . . .

Thought 1: *Someone* had been out in Vojvladimia. *Someone* had been asking all about Emerik Skulyevic. *Someone* had got hold of Mirna's wooden box.

Thought 2: Because of Thought 1, and because it now

turned out that our 'Mirna' was an imposter after all
(still couldn't quite get my head around that!), then it
seemed reasonable to suppose that Mirna and this Janet
Smith character were one and the same. She'd rooted
around for stuff in Vojvladimia, then travelled to the UK
and become Mirna. The timings seemed to fit, anyway.

Thought 3: Because of Thoughts 1 and 2, I couldn't
escape the creeping suspicion that maybe I'd been too
quick to dismiss the Elsa Moreaux connection. What was
Mirna's real identity? What was Janet Smith's real
identity? Could they both be the infamous leader of the
Minkstreet and Batt armed robbers?

My stomach did a quick backflip and went to hide
somewhere in my lower intestines. The possibility that
I'd have to confront one of the nastiest villains I'd ever
come across was deeply disturbing.

The only fly in the ointment, as they say, was that
same problem which had puzzled me earlier – how
could Mirna be Elsa Moreaux, since Elsa Moreaux –
constantly watched out for at airports, on ferries, etc, etc
– definitely left the country, definitely hadn't come back
again, and was probably still running a sushi bar in
Spain?

With a jolt of alarm, I suddenly realised that there *was*
a way for them to be the same person. Thinking back to
the contents of that wooden box Skull had shown me,

and thinking back to what Muddy had told me, I could see a way for Elsa Moreaux to have become both Janet Smith and Mirna Skulyevic. She *could* have returned to the UK, she *could* now be living in Skull's house – the house she herself had once lived in – and the idea filled me with horror.

Have you worked out how she might have done it?

I knew she'd been in contact with the skilled forger from Doyle Avenue. Since the real Mirna was dead, that newly issued passport that was in the wooden box must have been faked by the forger (a real passport can hardly be issued to a dead person!). Everything else in the box was real, but that passport must have been a fake.

And if the forger could create a fake passport in the name of Mirna Skulyevic, he could easily have created one in the name of Janet Smith. Both must have been good enough to fool the authorities, since the Mirna passport had all those border stamps in it (or, at least, it had leaving-Vojvladimia and entering-the-UK border stamps in it. The others could have been faked, but since 'Janet'/'Mirna' must have genuinely travelled from Vojvladimia to the UK at some point, those stamps were probably real).

The timetable would have gone like this: Elsa Moreaux gets two faked passports from the forger. She travels from Spain to Vojvladimia as 'Janet Smith'. The cops aren't looking for any Janet Smith, so she gets through without being noticed (although, I'd guess she has to adopt some sort of disguise to avoid face recognition computers).

As Janet Smith, she starts asking around about Emerik Skulyevic. She claims to be researching a biography. She manages to get hold of Mirna Skulyevic's wooden box.

She then travels to the UK, this time as Mirna. She now has with her enough proof to convince the Skulyevic family that she is the long-lost Mirna. After all, the only person in that house who's ever met Mirna before is Antonin, and he was only a young boy at the time, many years ago. 'Mirna' settles down in the Skulyevic's spare room. So far, so —

Wait! Wait! Wait!

Why would Elsa Moreaux do all that? *Why?*

Whichever way I looked at it, there was only one possible answer. There was only one reason Elsa Moreaux could have had for returning to her old home: that stolen gold was still in the house!

But the police had searched the place from top to bottom. They'd taken up all the floors. They'd dug up the garden. They couldn't possibly have missed several million pounds' worth of gold bullion! The idea was ridiculous. For a start, all that gold would take up quite a bit of space. It would be heavy, too.

And yet . . .

I retreated to my garden shed and my Thinking Chair. It was absolutely freezing in there, so I grabbed my notebook and a pen and retreated to underneath my bedsheets instead. By my flickering flashlight, I scribbled down a few ideas.

A Page From My Notebook

I'll approach this from Elsa Moreaux's point of view.

1. After years in prison, I get let out. Hee hee, I think, now I can retrieve that stolen gold.

2. I go to my old home, which is now Skull's home. Obviously, I already realise people will be living there, so I need a plan to get around them.

3. I find out that the people living there are called Skulyevic. Very unusual name. Doesn't take me long to discover who Emerik Skulyevic was, and that he left a sister behind when he fled Vojvladimia all those years ago.

4. The fact that Emerik has died gives me an idea. He was the last person who could have positively identified his long-lost sister, Mirna. Therefore, as long as I turn up with enough proof, then I can become Mirna and gain access to the house.

5. Under the watching eyes of the police, I leave the UK, having already got hold of a couple of fake passports through the Doyle Avenue forger guy. I go to Spain. I travel to Vojvladimia as Janet Smith, leaving the police thinking I'm still happily nibbling sushi.

And so on. That's all pretty clear now. However, I'm still left with two HUUUGE questions:

Question 1: WHY would Elsa go to all that trouble? She's a vicious armed robber. Why not simply bash in the door of the Skulyevic's house, and threaten them until she can retrieve the gold and leg it? That would be much more her style. Why all the sneakiness? What's stopping her just raiding the house as if it was a bank, just as she always did before?

Question 2: WHERE does the credit card thing come in? Why would Elsa need to go back to the Doyle Avenue guy and start dabbling in fake cards? It would surely be risky? Her cover could be blown!

Little did I know, but everything would become clear the following day at school. The final piece of the weirdly shaped puzzle which surrounded the Skulyevic family fell into place at last. All it took was a brief conversation with Skull himself.

'How's it going?' said Skull. The class was slowly traipsing in for the start of the school day and teachers were slowly traipsing along the corridors towards the staff room.

'Oh, er, not too bad,' I said, not quite knowing how to bring him up to date on all the worrying recent developments. 'Um, y'know, making progress . . .'

'So, you haven't actually found out any more about those credit cards?' asked Skull.

'Umm, not as such . . .' I said vaguely.

'Good!' said Skull. 'Because I think we can forget the whole thing now.'

'Huh? Why?'

'Her money's come through from her bank back in Vojvladimia,' said Skull cheerily. 'It occurred to me that she only got herself mixed up in stolen credit cards because she's been as short of cash as the rest of us at home. But now the problem's solved. I'm sure we'll see no more of that sort of thing from her. Let's just put it behind us, move on, forget the past and so on. Yes?'

'Ah,' I mumbled, going slightly red with

60

embarrassment. 'To be perfectly honest, um —'

'And she's done just what she said she'd do,' Skull went on. 'Remember, I told you, about how she was going to thank us for letting her stay? She's booked us a night at a hotel on the south coast. Plus train tickets for getting there, plus dinner, plus passes for Ocean Depths Aquarium. Isn't that nice of her?'

'Yes, now I think about it, you did mention it when you came to my shed,' I said. 'Can't have been cheap, all that for four people.'

'Three people,' said Skull. 'Mirna's staying at home. She says her gammy leg's playing up.'

As soon as Skull said that, the truth suddenly dawned on me. That final piece of the jigsaw clicked neatly into place and the picture was complete!

'She's not going!' I cried. 'Of course! What an idiot! I should have seen this from the very beginning! Skull, when are you and your parents off on this trip?'

'Tomorrow,' said Skull.

I almost squeaked with fright. 'Good grief! We have to act fast! Sorry, you can't go.'

'What? Why?'

I waggled my arms about in a bit of a panic. 'No. Scratch that. You *are* going —'

'Phew.'

'— but then you're coming straight back again!'

'What? Why?'

'Trust me! Say *nothing* to Mirna. *Nothing!* I mean it this time! Tomorrow morning, the three of you leave for the train station as arranged. I'll meet you halfway there and we'll all sneak back to your house.'

'No way – we'll miss the train!'

I wanted to jump up and down and make 'Ggnnnghh' noises. 'I promise you, you'd rather do things my way! We have to stop a serious crime being committed. Or rather, completed. And anyway, the three of you need to be there to . . . well, to find out what's been going on.'

'But Saxby . . .'

'Don't argue! I haven't a moment to lose! For a start, I need to go and see Muddy!'

Already, I was feeling nervous. I could have gone straight to the police with what I knew, but I felt it was important that Skull's family should see proof of what I'd discovered before the cops showed up. The truth was going to hurt them, but at least if they learned it for themselves it might not be quite so much of a shock. They deserved to find out about Mirna first, before any arrests were made!

The trouble was, doing the right thing for Skull's family also meant doing what I was dreading most: confronting the notorious Elsa Moreaux, face to face. The more I thought about it, the more my legs started to wobble.

I'd found the final piece of the puzzle thanks to three specific factors. There were three things which, considered alongside the weekend trip Skull had just told me about, added up to answer the questions that remained. Those factors were:

1) The negative results of the police's search of Skull's house, all those years ago.

2) The fact that Skull's house never used to have a garage. Or that hideous fireplace in the living room.

3) The way Skull's parents both worked and shopped from home.

How much of the puzzle have you pieced together?

CHAPTER
SEVEN

THE FOLLOWING MORNING, SKULL'S PARENTS were not happy bunnies. They weren't happy when Skull told them about my don't-catch-the-train plan. They weren't happy when Skull insisted they keep everything secret from Mirna. And they *really* weren't happy when I stood in the middle of the road, hands outstretched, blocking their car's way to the railway station. Happy bunnies, they were not.

'Listen, Saxby,' said Skull's dad with a sigh, 'I really don't want to hear any more of these wild stories.'

'We'll miss our train!' protested Skull's mum.

'Please, please, please do as I ask,' I pleaded. 'I know this seems mad, but it's also very, very important. If I'm right, you'll be glad you never went to the station. If I'm wrong, you'll only be delayed by an hour or so, you can catch the next train and you'll have my deepest apologies from now until the end of time. Deal?'

Reluctantly, they agreed. We all piled back into their car, and parked just out of sight of their house.

Keeping to one side of the street and stepping as softly as possible, the four of us made our way back towards Skull's house. A couple of net curtains twitched as neighbours wondered what we were up to, but apart from that everywhere was quiet.

I tapped at the small camera lens that was pinned to the front of my jacket. 'Muddy?' I whispered. 'All set?'

'Yup,' said a tinny voice in my ear. I adjusted the Whitehouse Listen-O-Scope Mark III that was curled around my right ear. 'Are you sure about this? It sounds potentially dangerous.'

'It *is* potentially dangerous,' I replied.

'So why couldn't I come too?' moaned Muddy. 'Spoilsport.'

'I need you to phone the police!' I hissed. 'Is this video feed live on Izzy's FaceSpace page or not?'

'Yes,' grumbled Muddy. 'I'll phone as soon as we get to the good bit. Hang on . . . Izzy's here. She says why not phone the police right now?'

'Because I don't want them finding out about this and turning up too early,' I said. 'Now shush. We're

65

nearly at Skull's house.'

'*We're* not the ones who need to shush,' mumbled Muddy grumpily. '*You're* the one who's *there*.'

I ignored him.

Slowly, Skull's parents, Skull and I sneaked across the front lawn of the house. There was no sign of movement inside.

'What if she sees us?' whispered Skull.

'She won't,' I whispered back. 'She'll be in the garage. But she might hear us, so shhhh.'

The four of us crept up to the garage. It had a swing-up-and-over metal door, which was very slightly open.

Suddenly, a sharp crack, like a hammer striking a nail, came from behind the garage door. Then another.

We looked at each other. Skull's parents couldn't quite believe what they were hearing.

The cracking came again, louder and heavier this time – more like a mallet being whacked down on to a hard surface. It sounded again and again, regularly, over and over. It stopped and started for the next few minutes until at last the garage fell quiet again.

Then we could hear scraping sounds, a grating noise and something crumbling on to the concrete floor inside. Finally, something clanked against metal.

I turned and nodded to Skull. He tiptoed to the far side of the garage door. We each took hold of one edge.

On my signal, we heaved the door up high. It clattered against the roof with a squeal of rusty springs.

Standing halfway down the garage was Mirna. She was wearing workman's overalls. In front of her, above a pile of loosened bricks and an assortment of tools, was a gaping hole in the wall which joined on to the house.

Behind her was a SuperSave trolley. In the trolley was a large, gleaming gold bar, about the size of a loaf of bread. In her hand was another one. Similar bars were stacked behind the hole.

She gaped at us. Her face showed a mixture of anger and surprise. For a split second, nobody moved.

'What on *Earth* . . .?!' cried Skull's dad.

Mirna dropped the gold brick she was holding into the trolley. She turned to face us again and this time the expression on her face was nothing less than pure fury.

'Hi there, Elsa Moreaux,' I said as casually as I could. Not casually at all, really – my voice was shaking like a nodding car mascot on a mountain trail.

She snorted. 'If you know who I am, you're sharper than the cops, I'll give you that.'

'Brilliant hiding place,' I said. 'Inside the wall cavity itself. The police would only have found it if they'd demolished the entire building.'

'Would someone please tell us *what* is going on?' cried Skull's dad.

I broke the news to them that Great Aunt Mirna wasn't Great Aunt Mirna after all. Briefly, I told them about the chain of clues in my investigation. 'I'm very sorry,' I added, 'but you've been conned from the outset.'

Elsa Moreaux picked up one of the bricks she'd removed from the wall and dropped it with a loud clack to the ground. I jumped with fright. She growled, 'Why didn't you send for the cops straight away?'

'That gold was still hidden,' I said. 'I was pretty sure it was in that wall, but I needed to wait. Until, that is, you went to fetch it yourself and showed me exactly where you'd put it.'

'And how could you possibly know it was inside this wall?' she spat. 'I made it perfect. It looked totally untouched!'

'Logical deduction,' I said. 'Your original plan, I think, was simply to turn up here as Mirna and stay just a day or two, until you had a chance to retrieve the gold. You couldn't simply burst in and grab it. Because of the way it was hidden, you needed a couple of hours in which to get the gold out. Which is why you decided to adopt a disguise.

'When you got out of prison, you worked out your plan: you went to Spain, then to Vojvladimia, then came back to the UK as Mirna Skulyevic. But when you finally got into the house you saw that Skull's dad had built a large, stone fireplace in the living room, on the other side of this wall – right over the top of your hiding place.

'That fireplace was far too thick and heavy to get through without major effort. You'd have to get to the hiding place from *this* side of the wall instead, from what had been the outside wall when *you* lived here. However, you had a piece of luck. There'd been another addition to the house – the garage. It would conceal you while you broke into the wall from *this* side instead.

'Unfortunately, your plan was upset by something else as well as the fireplace. Skull's parents were always at home. There was always somebody in the house. You'd assumed that it would only take a few days before you could grab an hour or two alone. It turned out that you might need weeks and weeks. So you had to outstay your welcome and you had to devise a way to get these three out of the house for a while.

'I can't be sure, but I guess that's why you went back to the guy in Doyle Avenue for credit cards – the one you'd got the fake passports from. You needed funds, yes?'

'Right,' snarled Elsa Moreaux. 'I came out of prison with barely anything and fake passports don't come cheap. Getting these dopes away for a day would soak cash I didn't have, so I had to do something.'

'And when the Doyle Avenue forger was arrested the

other day,' I said, 'you had to speed things up. If the police had got him, they might soon get you too. So you had to arrange for Skull's family to go on holiday straight away, this weekend. You had to get the gold as fast as possible, and by the time the Skulyevics came back and your cover was blown, you'd be safely away.

'It was clever of you to act a bit ditsy. That way, if the neighbours saw you pushing that SuperSave trolley down the street, with the gold hidden under a blanket, or a heap of rubbish, or something like that, they'd just think, *Uh-oh, there goes that batty old dear again.*'

Elsa Moreaux smiled at me. It made me shudder. It was nothing more than a lizard-like pull at her lips. 'You've covered all the angles, haven't you? Clever little boy. All the angles except one.'

'And what would that be?' I said, trying to keep my voice steady.

'If you know about me, you know about all the things I've done. All things I've been locked up for.' She picked up a long, hefty crowbar that she'd obviously used to help break into the wall. She weighed it in her hands, smiling that ghastly smile, never taking her eyes off me.

'You know I wouldn't hesitate,' she said quietly. 'I've got too much at stake here. This gold's worth nearly twenty million pounds today. You think I wouldn't cave your head in for twenty million? All your heads? You're

70

within striking distance already, boy. The rest of you, go over there, to the back of the garage.'

For a second, nobody moved. There was silence. Slowly, Elsa Moreaux raised the crowbar. Skull and his parents shuffled quickly aside, past the hole in the garage wall. I didn't dare move so much as an eyelid. My insides had turned runnier than school gravy and my throat felt like it was lined with sandpaper.

'Might be some time before you're all found,' said Elsa. She glared at me. 'Y'see, boy, all the angles except one.'

'Hmm, no,' I said, almost in a whisper. I tapped gently at the little lens attached to my jacket. 'I've got that one covered too.'

With a sudden screech of brakes, a police car skidded to a halt at the edge of the Skulyevics' front lawn. Another one shot into view behind it. Officers leaped out, yelling at Elsa Moreaux.

'Drop it! *Drop it!*'

I suddenly realised I hadn't taken a breath for about half a minute. I gasped shakily. Turning, I saw a familiar face getting out of a third car: Inspector Godalming, he of the whistling false teeth and the birdish walk, who I'd met during the case of *The Eye of the Serpent* (see volume five of my case files).

'Ssho, it's you again, shonny,' he sshaid, I mean said.

'You know I take a dim view of youngsh-ters interfering in poleesh invesh-tigations.'

I grinned up at him. 'Don't worry, I'll let you guys take all the credit. As ever.'

I had a great time the following Monday, basking in glory as Skull told the class about everything that had happened. Even our form tutor Mrs Penzler managed a few words of praise.

There was also one piece of good news – I'd found out that the bank that Elsa Moreaux's gang had stolen all that gold from had put up a reward at the time of the robbery. It had never been claimed, so Skull and his family found themselves able to afford a holiday after all.

I returned to my shed and my Thinking Chair. Skull had shared some of the reward money with me, so I bought a heater and kept it on full blast while I sat and jotted down some notes.

Case closed.

CASE FILE TWENTY-THREE:

DIAMONDS
ARE FOR
HEATHER

CHAPTER ONE

I SAW A MAGICIAN ON TV the other day. I don't normally like magic shows, I've never quite seen the point of them, but I'd been watching the previous programme and I couldn't be bothered to get up and hunt for the remote.

This particular show was live. The magician was going to see into the future (ooooh, spoooooky) and predict the six numbers that were going to come up on that night's Moneyspinner Lottery. The lottery would be drawn on another channel, and the magician had a TV set up showing the other channel's programmes (so you could flick back and forth and see that, yes, this trick was being done totally live).

Like I said, I don't normally rate magicians. It's so easy to see how they do it. But this trick sounded interesting. And, as it turned out, it was to play an important part in an investigation I've labelled *Diamonds Are for Heather*.

The Lottery trick went like this:

'First,' said the magician, 'I need six volunteers.' In the TV studio there were about two hundred people, plus a row filled with celebrities. Out to the front came a man with mad hair called Dave, a man with no hair at all called Keith, a very thin woman called Tracey and a very large woman called Barbara. There was also a sugary little girl called Donna (everyone went 'Ahhhhh'; I went 'Yeuchh'). Finally, from the celebs' seats, there was a TV reporter called Satnam – I'd often seen her reading the news and interviewing people in shopping centres.

Suspended behind the magician were six sets of plush red curtains, forming six little booths. They reminded me of a line of changing cubicles in a clothes shop.

Inside each booth was a chair and a table and on each table was a metal box and a padlock. Each volunteer sat down in one of the booths. Little Donna's feet didn't quite reach the floor. Everyone went 'Ahhhhh' again.

'Now,' said the magician, 'quiet please while I see into the future. A-ha! I see the six winning numbers!'

He went over to the first booth in the line of six, where Satnam the TV reporter was sitting. He took a piece of paper and a marker pen, wrote a number on the paper and gave the piece of paper to Satnam.

'Please fold up the paper and place it in the box,' he said. She placed it in the box. 'Now lock the box with the padlock!' She locked the box with the padlock. She handed him the key.

The magician repeated this all along the line. Little Donna giggled when she locked the box. Everyone went 'Ahhhhh' again. I looked around for a sick bucket.

Once he had all six padlock keys, the magician wheeled on a chunky-looking machine. He dropped the keys into the machine and it mangled them up.

'The predictions are safely under lock and key,' he said. He drew the front curtains of each booth. We could still see the volunteers' feet poking out. Little Donna's shoes were just visible, swinging away happily. Aaaaah, yeuchh, etc, etc.

Down from above came six cameras. Each one pointed into a booth. Six small video rectangles appeared along the bottom of my TV screen. 'Give us a wave,' said the magician. All the volunteers looked up and waved at the camera.

By now, there was less than a minute to go to the lottery draw. There was a lot of tension building in the TV studio.

'Six numbers will be drawn,' declared the magician. 'Each of those numbers I have predicted. Each number is in a locked box. The keys to those boxes have been destroyed. The boxes are being guarded by our six volunteers. You at home are watching our six volunteers on the overhead cameras. My predictions cannot be accessed, touched, removed, changed or altered in any way.'

He turned up the sound on the TV showing the other channel. The draw took place. The six booths and the six camera feeds were visible all the time. The lottery numbers drawn were . . . 6, 34, 102, 7, 19, and 85.

The magician swept open the six curtains. 'Out you come, bring the boxes, give 'em a big hand, everyone!'

A hefty-looking guy with a hammer and chisel appeared from backstage. With a couple of clanking blows he broke open the padlock on the first box. 'I've got him on loan from the ballet,' said the magician, smiling. Laughter all round.

The magician asked Satnam to open the box, take out the paper and show us the number written on it.

It was a 6. The look on Satnam's face was pure noooo-waaaay.

Smash! 'Box number two, please.' It was a 34. Gasps and whoops.

Box number three, 102. Number four, a 7. Number five, a 19. Finally, little Donna opened box number six.

'What number do you think it's going to be?' said the magician.

'Eighty . . . ffffive?' muttered Donna, wide-eyed.

Yup, it was. Little Donna jumped up and down squealing. Everyone else erupted in cheers.

The magician turned to the camera and said, 'Y'know, in all the excitement, I forgot to buy a lottery ticket! D'oh!'

Laughter and applause.

I was genuinely baffled. I'd seen tricks with vanishing elephants and tricks with young ladies falling into loads of pieces and I'd usually seen through them in a couple of minutes. But this one really got me thinking.

It wasn't until I was lying in bed that night, unable to sleep, mulling the whole thing over, that the truth finally dawned on me. I'd been looking at the problem in totally the wrong way. Because the result of the trick had been so apparently impossible, I'd been coming up with all kinds of complicated explanations (mucking around with the whole country's signals for the other TV channel, putting tiny, dissolving printers in the boxes, that sort of stuff) when all I needed to do was remember that some tricks – like some crimes – rely on very simple ideas.

The Lottery Prediction trick was performed with . . .

No, wait. Perhaps you've already worked it out for yourself? It depended on three things:

1. Keys are easily duplicated.

2. Video is easily looped. (Show three unchanging seconds of an empty street over and over again and it'll look like hours of empty street!)

3. People lie.

Have you spotted how it was done?

The magician wrote nothing on those pieces of paper. Not one teeny tiny scribble. Certainly not the correct lottery draw numbers. He just pretended.

Why? He didn't need to write anything. All six volunteers, including Satnam the well-known celebrity and Donna the little girl nobody would suspect in a million years, were in on it.

The magician picked his six 'volunteers'. 'Sit inside these curtained booths,' he said. 'You can guard the boxes. We'll watch you all the time using these cameras.'

Suppose you were one of those six:

The magician gets you to put a piece of paper into the box on the table in front of you. You lock the box and give him the key.

The curtain closes. You sit absolutely still for five seconds or so. Enough time for the technical people operating the cameras to loop the video. Yes, the TV crew are in on it as well. Once there are a few seconds recorded of you sitting still, it can be looped around and around and anyone looking at it will simply see you sitting there.

Now, you mustn't move your feet. Remember, the people in the studio can see your feet under the curtain. They look at your feet, they look at the looped video and they are totally convinced that you are sitting still, guarding the box on the table in front of you, exactly as you are told to.

The real lottery draw takes place. The magician turns up the sound on the TV outside so you can hear what's going on.

Suppose you're, say, third in the line. You listen out for the third winning number. In this case 102. From up your sleeve (or down your jumper, or wherever) you produce a duplicate key to the box in front of you, a key you've had hidden since before the whole show started. You quietly unlock the padlock, open the box and take out the folded paper the magician gave you.

Remembering to keep your feet still, you then take a marker pen from up your sleeve (or down your jumper, or wherever), and write the relevant number – in this case 102 – on to the paper. You need to write it in a handwriting style that's been agreed on, maybe practised, by all of you, so that all the numbers look the same and people will believe the magician wrote them.

You place the paper back in the box and re-fasten the padlock. A few seconds later, off go the cameras, back goes the curtain and out you come.

The magician now has six boxes, containing six numbers which exactly match the winning lottery draw. All that stuff with the hammer and chisel is just dramatic window dressing.

Easy peasy. All you have to do now is act amazed and surprised when your box is opened, and the magician looks like he's done something incredible.

Of course, the simple Lottery Prediction trick couldn't have been further from my mind when *Diamonds Are for Heather* first came my way. I was in my Crime HQ – the garden shed – when it started.

I was doing two things: searching through my case files and shivering. No, three things: searching, shivering and hoping that the batteries in my flashlight would last another couple of minutes. It was already beginning to splutter and fade slightly. It wasn't quite five in the afternoon, but the icy shroud of winter gloom that had engulfed the town was already darker than a black cat in a coal mine. The heater I'd recently bought for the shed had packed up.

I was looking for information I needed to put in the book I was planning. I'd decided it was time for Saxby Smart, brilliant schoolboy detective, to share his insights into the criminal mind with the world.

Grumble, grumble where is it? . . . Moan, grumble, bloomin' freezing in here . . . Grumble [*chattering teeth*] . . . Ought to get a proper light for this shed . . . [*shiver*] Grumble and some bloomin' heating . . . Moan, whinge, the things I do for truth and justice . . .

Suddenly, my phone bleeped loudly. I almost knocked the flashlight off my desk in fright. Shadows bounced madly off the pile of DIY and gardening stuff that took up half the shed.

Pausing only to grumble some more about people texting me when I was in the middle of grumbling, I opened my inbox and read, *I have a case for you. Will you help me?*

There was no name attached, and I didn't recognise the number. I texted back, *Who are you? Bit busy. Can we talk at school tomorrow?*

At last I found the file I was looking for and tucked it under my arm. Just as I was starting to shiver again and wishing I'd worn my woolly hat, the reply arrived: *No. Doesn't matter who I am. Case is urgent. Will you help me or not?*

I paused at the shed door, frowning slightly at the message glowing up at me from the tiny screen.

Hmmm.

CHAPTER
TWO

THIS TEXTING BACK AND FORTH between me and a mysterious someone else continued for a while. During that time, I left the shed, warmed up indoors, made myself something to eat, went to the loo, brushed my teeth and got ready for bed.

The conversation went like this:

Me: *Sure, I want to help. But must know who you are!*

Other: *Told you – name not relevant. Help or not?*

Me (after some thought): *Tell me about your problem. But I'm not promising anything!*

Other: *Read attached file.*

The attached file read:

A diamond smuggling operation has been recently tracked across South America and Western Europe. Check the news feeds if you want more information. Various security forces from several countries are involved. The smugglers currently believe they have outwitted the authorities. They are using a series of one-off meetings to pass diamonds from one criminal organisation to another. The next such meeting will take place at the Regal Hotel on Saturday. One of the smugglers, codenamed Moss, will book into the hotel at six that evening. His contact, codenamed Heather, will meet him there at 9 p.m. Neither of them knows the other. A reliable source of information at the hotel has overheard the maintenance man, Bryan Beeks, talking to an unknown person by phone. Beeks is thought to have links with several high-profile criminals. He has learned of the smugglers' meeting and is planning to steal the diamonds before they can be handed over. The smugglers are unaware of his plan. You must keep a close watch on Beeks and prevent him from stealing the diamonds. The smugglers are not your concern. Will you help?

I read the file through a couple of times. I wasn't sure what to make of it. The Regal was the poshest hotel in town. I'd never been inside it before, but I knew where it was. It occurred to me that the mysterious texter might be playing some kind of trick. It was a possibility which lurked darkly at the back of my mind until the case was all but solved. However, I'll tell you now that trickery was the last thing on this person's mind.

I had only one clue to their identity. It wasn't so much

what they'd said, as the fact that they'd said it at all. Remember that – it'll be important. This single, vague clue would, it turned out, nag at me for days.

Eventually, I replied: *OK. Will see what I can do. But don't expect to remain anonymous!*

A Page From My Notebook

My mystery texter. Who could he or she be?

He or she mentioned the online news. Could they be a journalist, a news reporter? Possible!

He or she mentioned security services. Could they be from the Government? Highly unlikely!

He or she mentioned an informer at the hotel. Could they themselves be this informer? Also possible!

One more possibility – COULD HE/SHE BE ONE OF THE SMUGGLERS? Wouldn't the smugglers be the first people who'd want this Beeks character out of the way? Could they be lying about the whole 'security forces' thing and simply want someone to remove a thorn in their side?

What do I do?

Whoever the texter is, he/she already knows who I am and what I do.

If the texter is one of the good guys, then fine. But if they're one of the bad guys . . . ? Could I end up working for the wrong side? Will I even be able to know WHICH side I'm working for, unless I identify this texter?

I must be CAREFUL!

CHAPTER THREE

AFTER A LOT OF THOUGHT, and a lack of sleep, I decided that the best course of action was to proceed as planned and, er, hope for the best!

One result of all that thinking was a brilliant idea for how to carry out my investigations without raising suspicion. After all, you don't see all that many schoolboy detectives wandering around the average hotel, now, do you? I'd thought of the perfect way in – Susan Lillington.

Susan, who was in the other class in my year group at St Egbert's School, had not just one parent who worked at the Regal, but two. I remembered her talking about it, ages ago, to my great friend Isobel 'Izzy' Moustique, that Rani of all Research and official Chief Brainbox of St

Egbert's. (Readers of my earlier case files will know that some of Izzy's enormous family were also in the hotel trade.)

As I arrived at school the next morning, I hurried over to Susan. Maybe, I thought, *she* was the mystery texter?

'Hi Saxby,' she said, 'what's up?'

'Um, well, that's just what I was going to ask you,' I said.

She gave me a blank look. 'How do you mean?'

'You've not come across any crimes?' I asked. 'You've not, oooh, I dunno, sent any texts recently?'

She gave me a look as blank as a fresh sheet of A4. 'What are you talking about?'

The texter really wasn't her, then!

'Oh, nothing! I've got a favour to ask you.'

'Yes?' she said.

'I'm investigating a case at the moment, and on Saturday evening I need to be at the hotel your parents work at, the Regal. Do you think you could arrange some sort of cover story? I'm there doing work experience for a school project, that sort of thing?'

She grinned. 'No need! I'm going to be there on Saturday anyway with some friends. You can come along with us, if you like.'

'Great!' I said. 'Couldn't be better!'

Her eyes darted around. 'What's the case about,

Saxby?' she whispered. 'Is it dangerous?'

'I hope not!' I cried, going slightly pale. 'I need to keep an eye on some diamond smugglers.'

'Smugglers!' she squealed. 'Diamonds! Hey, that's really exciting!'

'It's not a game,' I said, in a serious tone of voice.

She cleared her throat and sloped her fingers into a couple of nice-and-calm gestures. 'Yes, right.' She fought back a giggle.

'See you later,' I tutted.

I just had time before lessons to have a word with my other great friend, George 'Muddy' Whitehouse, that Maharajah of Mechanics and official Top Gadgethead of St Egbert's. Half his breakfast was littered down the front of his school uniform.

'Just the bacon and beans this morning, was it?' I said. 'Your mum out of eggs?'

'Yeah,' he gasped, shaking his head in amazement. 'You really are the greatest detective.'

I gave him my phone. 'Could you take a look at this for me? I got some anonymous texts last night, from a number I didn't recognise, and I need to find out more about the sender.'

Muddy turned the phone over a couple of times in his bike-oil-stained hands. 'Hmm, not going to be easy.'

'Because the sender would have covered their tracks?'

'No, because your phone's such a piece of junk. Something more up to date might capture more metadata, but a basic model like this . . .' He wrinkled his nose and sniffed. 'Nah, you'd have to hack too far into the SIM card. I keep telling you, I can upgrade this for you!'

'No thanks.'

'Bigger battery pack, better electronics, touch screen. You've seen the Whitehouse Connect-U-Fast III, my latest invention? Thingummy over in Mrs Whatsit's class has got one and he swears by it.'

'He swears *at* it,' I said. 'It hardly fits in his pocket.'

'Yeah, but it's a good phone,' said Muddy. 'Goes six weeks between charges.'

'Who needs six weeks' talk time?' I said. 'Unless you're trekking up the Amazon. And then you wouldn't get a signal.'

'You never know!' protested Muddy. 'You might need it for whatever investigation you're on right now! What investigation *are* you on right now?'

I gave him a brief summary of events so far. I missed out the bit about the security forces. Telling Muddy that spies were involved would be like letting a toddler eat its own weight in sugar.

'Are you free this weekend?' I asked. 'In case I need your help on something technical?'

'This would be at the Regal?'

'Yes.'

'Saturday?'

'Yes.'

'Susan Lillington?'

'Yes.'

'No way.'

'Why? What's wrong with Susan Lillington?' I asked.

'Nothing whatsoever,' said Muddy, 'on a normal day. Saturday is her birthday.'

'Oh! She didn't tell me that,' I repeated.

'These friends she's having over are all girls.'

'Oh! She didn't tell me that,' I said.

'They're having a girlie sleepover.'

'Oh! She didn't . . . What? *What?*'

'Izzy told me,' said Muddy. 'And you've just invited yourself along, have you? Hmm, good luck with that, then.'

He handed me back my phone. I was too shocked to move.

CHAPTER FOUR

BY FRIDAY AFTERNOON, THE ICY swirls which had been circling the town for days finally descended into a thick covering of snow. Everything outside took on an eerie, artificial look. In the winter half-light, the streets seemed lit only by the reflections off the snowy pavements. People stepped carefully, taking care not to slip, huddled tightly into overcoats and scarves.

The Regal Hotel was a broad, three-storey building on the long, straight road which glanced off the eastern edge of the town. It had been built in the middle of the eighteenth century as a coaching inn where travellers going north and south across the country could stop and change horses.

The hotel was set out in a kind of giant U-shape, with

the bottom of the 'U' formed by the narrow front section facing the street and the two sides forming a large central courtyard. Two hundred years ago, this paved courtyard would have been filled with wooden coaches and ladies in long skirts. And probably quite a lot of horse poo, come to think of it. That Saturday, however, it was the site of tastefully arranged pots forming an ornamental garden – a garden covered in snow.

It was dark by the time I arrived. Orange lamps on short poles shone a distinctly creepy glow over the small area marked *Staff Car Park* that I crossed on my way into the building, my wellies crunching against the snow. With a smile, I noticed that my footprints were the only marks at this end of the car park, except for a set of widely-spaced, striding steps which led into the hotel from a battered old purple van.

Entering through the shiny glass doors that faced the road, I felt like a caveman suddenly transported into the twenty-first century from a frozen wasteland. Inside, the place was blissfully warm, cheerfully bright and so thickly carpeted that you couldn't hear a single footstep.

Signs on the opposite wall pointed visitors either to the left for the hotel's restaurant, La Splendide, or to the right for the hotel's reception. I went right.

Being the depths of winter, it was low season for the hotel and there were relatively few guests.

Susan and several other girls, including Izzy, were gathered by the reception desk. Izzy was in her normal out-of-school gear – all chunky rings, bright colours and glittery fringes. The girls and I exchanged a criss-cross of 'hello's and 'hi's.

'Saxby, is it?' said the tall, smartly dressed woman behind the reception desk.

'This is my mum,' explained Susan. 'Mel. She's on duty at the front desk all evening.'

'Hello, Susan's mum,' I said. 'Um, I do just want to make it clear, I don't do girlie sleepovers. I'm here in my official capacity as brilliant schoolboy detective. I'm undercover. I'm going home as soon as possible. I don't do girlie sleepovers.'

Mel gave me the same blank look Susan had given me at school. 'Right,' she said slowly. 'OK.' Something in her expression said, 'Yes, you're every bit as odd as I expected'. She brightened up with a snap and said, 'Why don't you all wait in the administration office until the last two arrive?'

Behind the reception desk were two offices, one marked *Administration* and the other marked *Supervisor*. Into the admin office we trooped. It was a large, cluttered room with one desk against the wall close to the door and another two over by the window. Through the window's slatted blinds, I could see the hotel's big, snow-covered courtyard, and beyond that the other 'arm' of the hotel's U-shape with an enormous window.

'That's the restaurant,' said Susan. 'We'll be going over there to eat in a little while.'

'Your dad works here too, doesn't he?' I asked, watching a fresh drifting of snow glide gently down outside.

'Yes, he's the restaurant's chef,' said Susan. 'He'll be cooking our dinner tonight. He used to be in the police, years ago, but Mum kept worrying that one day he'd come home with a bullet wound. Then one day he came home with a stab wound and she made him quit. I think he prefers cooking.'

'Fair enough,' I said with a smile.

'Pressies!' announced Izzy. There was a sudden flurry of ribbons and wrapping paper and female activity.

Earlier in the day, I'd considered not bringing a birthday present with me, because I wanted it to be absolutely clear that I don't do girlie sleepovers. However, it would have been rude not to. So I added my small parcel to the pile.

While the girls were oooh-ing and ahhhh-ing all over the place, I took a look around the office. There were cardboard boxes stacked here and there, and a couple of scribbled-on flip charts. Above me hung a projector – exactly the same sort of thing as we had in our classroom at school. That and the flip charts told me that this room must be used for staff training.

Izzy appeared at my shoulder. 'Aww, are you feeling a bit of a spare part?'

'Pack it in,' I muttered.

At that moment, a man wearing a Regal Hotel sweatshirt came clattering into the room. His hair was yanked back into a ponytail and he had a beard which looked like a small mammal clinging to the underside of his face. He had a laptop under one arm and was hobbling along with the help of a grey metallic walking stick.

'Hello, Mr Beeks,' said Susan.

'Oh, yes, happy birthday, Susan,' he replied with a nod.

Ah, Bryan Beeks! The maintenance man who was my reason for being here in the first place.

'Thanks,' said Susan. 'We'll be out of your way soon, we're just waiting for another two to arrive.'

Luckily, I hadn't mentioned any details of my investigation to Susan, beyond what I'd told her at school. She had no idea that I was keeping a close eye on this guy.

I was struck by Mr Beeks's voice. It was distinctively deep, and he had a noticeable Geordie accent. Whoever it was at the hotel who was the 'reliable source of information' the texter had mentioned, I was now fairly sure they wouldn't have mistaken Beeks's voice for anyone else's. So far so good.

'You'll have to be out of here soon, I'm afraid,' said Mr Beeks. 'I've booked this room all evening, I've got a lot of paperwork to get done. I've let it pile up a bit.'

'How's your leg?' asked Susan.

'Not too bad,' he said, propping his walking stick against the desk and shuffling over to the nearest seat. 'The doctor says it'll be another few weeks before it's healed.'

He seemed calm and friendly, not at all like someone who was planning to stage a diamond heist within the next couple of hours. He snapped his fingers and stood up again. 'I've left my phone in my coat pocket.'

He limped across the room. I picked up his walking stick and handed it to him. It was quite thick, but very light.

'Shall I fetch the phone for you?' said Susan. 'If your leg's hurting?'

'Bless you,' he said, smiling at her, 'but it's only in the staff cloakroom down the hall. Won't be a minute.'

Out he went, leaving his laptop on the desk. The last couple of sleepover guests arrived and Susan finished opening her pressies. There was a hushed moment when she got to mine, a copy of a *really* good book I'd read recently called *True Tales of Gruesome Crimes*. Izzy gave me a stare, which I think was her way of signalling that I'd chosen well.

It turned out that Susan's sleepover party were

staying in one of the unbooked rooms on the third floor. She got the keycard from her mum at reception and we all charged up to room 307. Nice: more thick carpet, big TV, and a shiny white bathroom so big you'd need to mount an expedition to reach the toilet.

Meanwhile, I was torn between not wanting to get involved in all the girlie talk going on, and needing to make progress with my enquiries.

'Mr Beeks, he does the fixing of broken stuff around here, yes?' I asked casually.

'Yes, he's such a nice guy,' said Susan.

'What's with the walking stick?'

'He's torn the ligaments in his ankle and knee, playing rugby. But he's still coming into work. Did you see his crappy old purple van in the car park?'

'Yes, I did,' I chuckled.

Yes. I did.

I'd suddenly spotted an important clue. Bryan Beeks hadn't torn the ligaments in his ankle and knee at all! That injury was nothing more than acting!

Think back to what I saw before coming into the hotel. Have you spotted the same mismatch I had?

Apart from my own, there had been only one set of footprints in that snowy staff car park. They'd come from an old purple van, which I now knew to be Bryan Beeks's. They'd shown someone striding across the snow. Something that would have been impossible if he'd really hurt his leg as badly as he claimed.

But why would anyone pretend to have an injured leg? How could that have any bearing on the robbery he was supposed to be planning? Was he going to make the smugglers think he couldn't run away from them, or something? It didn't appear to make any sense. However, the mysterious texter had been right – keeping watch on Beeks was obviously a good idea.

The girls were having a great time. One or two were sniffing approvingly at the free shampoo in the bathroom, but most of them were lounging around pretending to order fizzy cocktails or flicking through channels on the TV. I took a peek inside the mirrored wardrobe.

'Hey, there's a room safe,' I said.

I heard a rapid scrambling behind me. They all crowded in to have a look.

'Hey, there's a room safe,' they said. It was quite a large one, with a numeric keypad lock, and was bolted to the wall at the back of the wardrobe.

'All the rooms have them,' said Susan. 'You can set

your own combination. Shall we put our stuff in there while we go to dinner?'

There was a chorus of 'Yeah!'s. Every last one of them went straight to their overnight bag, and took out a phone and a handheld games console. After a few bleeps of its keypad, the safe held enough technology to stock a small shop!

By then it was past seven o'clock, and we were all hungry. Susan led us back down past reception, along the corridor-like front of the building, and into the other half of the hotel's U-shape, on the far side of the courtyard.

A sleazy-looking, greasy-faced beanpole in a black jacket and bowtie greeted us at the entrance to La Splendide. This, it turned out, was Vernon, the head waiter. He eyed us as if we were a pack of scuttering cockroaches.

'You're at one of the window tables, Miss Lillington,' he said to Susan, as if he was speaking to something a cockroach might turn its nose up at.

The restaurant was positively beautiful. The dining area was large and delicately laced with the smell of fresh bread. Its high ceiling was decorated with flowery patterns, and the lighting came from shaded lamps placed at the centre of every table.

Our table was circular, spread with a spotless white

tablecloth and neatly laid with sparkling cutlery and tall glasses. It was placed beside that big window I'd seen from the office earlier on; looking out, I could see across the snowy courtyard to the brightly lit rectangle of the office's window. The blinds were open now, and Bryan Beeks was clearly visible, sitting at the desk by the door, working at his laptop.

I had the perfect vantage point from which to watch him. As I sat down, next to Izzy, Susan leaned across to me and whispered, 'Spotted any diamond smugglers yet?'

Ah! Good point!

'Excuse me a minute,' I said, 'just got to verify something.'

I nipped back out to the reception desk. There was now a *Do Not Disturb* sign on the admin office door, and I could very faintly hear Bryan Beeks tapping away at his laptop inside.

I asked Susan's mum if I could take a quick look at the hotel register, as part of my ongoing detective investigation into certain matters which would have to remain confidential for the time being. She smiled sweetly and clearly thought I was slighty peculiar. Anyway, the current screen of the register showed all check-ins for that day:

TIME	NAME & ADDRESS	ROOM
4.22 p.m	G.T. Foreman 145 Bailey Street, Bath	209
4.40 p.m.	Mr & Mrs Smith c/o GPL Ltd, Poole, Dorset	206
5.09 p.m.	Peter Glynn Flat 2, Bunn Court, Stortley	319
5.58 p.m.	Mr L. Moss 12 Watford Grove, Leamington	217
6.30 p.m.	Daniel West The Priory, Totley, Glos	222
6.33 p.m.	Louise Draper 38 Murray Road, Birmingham	301

I hurried back to La Splendide. It was seven twenty-five p.m. and, besides Susan's group, there were about half a dozen people dotted around the restaurant. I slid back into my seat. Everyone was looking at menus.

'Any news?' asked Izzy.

'Yes,' I said. 'I can at least confirm that the first of tonight's two smugglers has arrived and which room he's in.'

It had taken only a brief look at the register to spot the smuggler. Have you worked out who it was?

'Only one person arrived at around six, the time the texter told me the first smuggler would get here. I'm pretty sure that's him because he's using the name Moss, which also ties in with what I was told. I doubt either the name or the address he put down are genuine. Anyway, he's in Room 217, which if I'm not mistaken puts him on the floor above where we are now. I'm not sure what time his contact will arrive, the one codenamed Heather, but they're due to meet at nine o'clock. Let's see thaaaaat's . . . exactly an hour and a half from now.'

'By the way,' said Izzy, 'I checked the online news services, like you asked. There are indeed several articles about a smuggling operation. There are very few details, but they appear to back up what Mr Mystery said.'

'Or Mrs Mystery,' I added.

'Or Mrs Mystery, right.'

Vernon the waiter slimed up to the table and asked if everyone had chosen what they wanted to eat. He made it sound as if we were selecting clumps of goo out of a gutter. Hurriedly, I picked up a menu.

While the others were ordering variations on the theme of whatever-sounds-poshest, I kept glancing out of the window. Bryan Beeks was there, in the office across the courtyard, tapping away.

I was just trying to work out what *Soup du Jour* might mean, when a movement caught my eye. I glanced back across the courtyard and saw Beeks limping over to the office window. He reached up and shut the blinds.

'Sir?'

'Huh?' I said.

'Are you ready to order, sir?' sighed Vernon.

'Oh! Ummm . . .'

I returned my gaze to the window. The blinds were open again. Beeks was back at his desk, working away for all the world to see.

'Sir?'

'Oh! Sorry!' I said. 'Er, have you got any curry?'

'As it's a special occasion, sir, I'm sure Chef can oblige,' said Vernon.

'Oh great, I'll have that, then. Thanks,' I said with a grin.

Once Vernon had oozed away to the kitchen, all the others at the table stared at me.

'Curry?' said Izzy quietly.

'I like curry,' I said, even more quietly.

The restaurant was getting slightly busier now. Our table was rippling with chatter.

I wondered why Beeks had shut those blinds for, what was it, no more than thirty seconds? Was he signalling to someone? However, as he was clearly carrying on with his work, I let the matter pass. Maybe he liked to have as good a view of the restaurant as the restaurant had of him?

Within a minute of each other, two people entered the restaurant who grabbed my attention. The first was a tall, neatly clipped man in a spotless black suit. Vernon indicated a table towards the back of the room, but the man asked if he could sit closer to the entrance.

He grabbed my attention because I could have sworn I knew him from somewhere. I couldn't quite work out why.

I nudged Izzy. 'That guy over there, the one in the black suit,' I whispered. 'I'm sure I've seen him before. Does he ring any bells with you?'

'Nope.' Izzy shrugged. 'He could just be someone you've seen in a shop, or something like that.'

'Hmm,' I muttered. 'Dunno.'

The second person to grab my attention appeared. This was a much shorter man, wearing a light brown leather jacket. His face had more lines than a school exercise book and was topped with a messy thatch of ginger hair.

This one caught my attention for a totally different reason. As Vernon approached him and asked if he was a hotel guest or just visiting the restaurant, the man replied that he was in room 217.

I nudged Izzy again. 'That's the smuggler. Moss.'

Izzy nudged Susan and whispered in her ear.

'Ooooh,' whispered Susan, leaning over to me. 'Do

you think his pockets are loaded with diamonds?'

'No, I'm sure the diamonds will have been put in the safe in his room,' I whispered, switching my gaze nervously between Moss, Black Suit Man and Beeks over in his office. 'Otherwise, why book a room at all? He could simply meet his contact here in the restaurant. No, I expect he'll be worried about being ambushed by rival crooks. The diamonds will be locked away.'

Moss seemed to be deep in conversation with Vernon the waiter. He brandished a bright red slip of paper at Vernon, which Vernon took, read, handed back, took again and finally walked off with, looking slightly puzzled.

'What's that paper?' I whispered to Susan. 'I'm sure I saw the hotel's logo on it.'

'That's an ACV,' whispered Susan, looking as puzzled as Vernon.

'A what?'

'Sorry, that's just what Mum and Dad call them. Awkward Customer Vouchers. They get given out when hotel guests have had loads of things go wrong. Luggage missing, forgotten wake-up calls, that sort of thing. It gives them a free dinner here in the restaurant. Goodness knows why he'd have one, he's only just got here.'

'He couldn't have been given one by your mum when he checked in?' I said.

'No way,' said Susan. 'Dad says they can cost the hotel a small fortune because whenever someone gets given one they go mad and eat all the most expensive stuff on the menu. Only the real moaners ever get one.'

Moss was busy giving Vernon the waiter a long list of main courses and side orders. Meanwhile, I noticed Black Suit Man, who'd been sitting quietly waiting for his starter to arrive, get up and walk out.

I looked over at Beeks in his office, then back at Moss. Vernon was on to a second page in his waiter's jotter.

Wait a minute! There *was* a reason Moss might have had that voucher. And it had nothing to do with having made a complaint.

Based on what I'd just been talking about with Izzy and Susan, and on what I'd been told was going to happen that evening, I could see part of a plan lurking behind that voucher. There was a clear reason for Moss having it.

Can you work out what I was thinking?

Those diamonds were locked away in room 217. If someone was going to steal them, they would want to find a way to get Moss out of his room for a while. What better way than if he had one of those vouchers? Beeks could slip it under the door of Moss's room – a simple complimentary-hotel-welcome-thingummy. Moss would then be down in the restaurant while —

'— Beeks sneaks up to 217 and nicks the diamonds. He's the maintenance man. He can easily over-ride the lock on the room safe!' I hissed.

'Sorry, did you say something?' said Izzy.

I almost yelped. I whipped around in my seat, expecting to see the office across the courtyard empty. Beeks would be on his way upstairs right now!

But . . .

No. There he was. As before. Working away at his laptop. He turned to check through some papers and I could see his face clearly.

'You OK, Saxby?' Izzy asked.

I turned back to where Moss was giving Vernon the waiter a long list of food orders. Something was going on here. Something I couldn't quite see yet.

Everyone at our table turned round as a distant crashing sound came echoing along the corridor from reception. One or two restaurant diners gave a miniature cheer.

'Sounds like Mum's having trouble at the front desk,' said Susan.

I leaped to my feet. I was starting to feel nervous – something was *definitely* going on here. 'I'll go and check. Izzy, watch Mr Beeks over there. Don't take your eyes off him!'

I hurried out of La Splendide and along the corridor to the reception area. On the way, I passed Black Suit Man heading back towards the restaurant. *Where* did I know that guy from?

At reception, Susan's mum had just finished re-filling the display stand that was propped up beside the welcome desk. It was one of those stack-up things which holds fold-out leaflets advertising local attractions and places to eat.

'What was that crash?' I asked.

'This display thing going over!' said Susan's mum. 'Some clumsy clot comes along, asks if we've got a local map and he manages to knock all my leaflets flying. Never mind, no harm done.'

'A guy in a black suit?' I asked.

'Yes,' said Susan's mum.

Two things rang an alarm bell in my head. No, three things!

One: Black Suit Man hadn't appeared to be carrying any map with him on his way back to the restaurant.

111

Two: That display stand was quite chunky. It would take a *really* clumsy clot to knock it over.

Three: The *Do Not Disturb* sign on the admin office door behind the reception desk was slightly askew.

Something was *definitely* going on here!

'Has Mr Beeks come out of that office?' I asked.

'No,' said Susan's mum.

'Are you absolutely sure?'

'Yes! Why? Listen, you can hear him typing.'

It was true. I could, just about, hear the tapping of laptop keys.

'I'm sure he won't mind if I pop in and ask him something,' I said.

'Oh yes he would,' said Susan's mum, raising a warning hand. 'He's behind on paperwork and he's asked that nobody interrupt him.'

'Yes, but —'

'But nothing. Several members of staff need to book that office from time to time to catch up on things and we all respect each other's catch-up time.'

I had so many alarm bells going off in my head, I could hardly think straight. I decided to take a look at room 217. I'd be taking a big risk. What if Moss came back to his room? But a lot was at stake. What if the diamonds had already gone and I was too late? What if a robbery was going on right under my nose?

I ran up the wide staircase which led to the upper floors, the thick carpeting absorbing every footstep. The silence around me as I ran made the anxious thumping of my heart feel all the more severe. Although that may partly have been down to how unfit I am. By the time I got upstairs, I was out of breath. I really *must* get more exercise.

Without the slightest pause, I flung open the fire door at the top of the stairs and hurtled along the tastefully lit – *WHUMP!*

I ran into Bryan Beeks so hard that we both bounced backwards. I landed with a thud on my bottom. For a fraction of a second, we stared at each other in a daze. Beeks slapped both hands to his leg.

'Owwww! My leg! Oww! Watch where you're going, young man! That hurt!'

'S-Sorry!' I stuttered. Then I came to my senses and thought, *What am I saying? It's an act!*

Beeks staggered to his feet, rubbing at his leg and wincing. 'Holy moley, what are you doing running around like that? You're one of Susan Lillington's friends, aren't you?'

'Yes. Sorry. Er, rushing to the loo. About to burst. Got my best trousers on.'

I picked up his heavy walking stick and handed it back to him. Then I turned and ran back the way I'd come.

My mind felt as if a swarm of bees had been let loose inside it. Bryan Beeks was upstairs! Bryan Beeks, the guy I'd been warned was planning to steal the diamonds! What had he just been up to? Where was he going? Where had he been?

I'd just seen Bryan Beeks.

But . . . wasn't Bryan Beeks in the admin office?

I scuttled past reception. ('Hi!' I waved to Susan's mum. She smiled flatly. She obviously thought I was a bit strange.) I scooted back into the restaurant, just in time to see everyone at my table finishing their soup.

'Saxby, there you are!' cried Susan. 'Where have you been?'

'Getting my mind boggled,' I muttered.

As I sat down, a phone started warbling. Black Suit Man snapped open a tiny handset from his top pocket.

I turned to look out of the window, across the courtyard. Bryan Beeks was working away in the office, just as he had been before.

'Did you watch him?' I whispered to Izzy.

'Yes,' said Izzy. 'He hasn't budged.'

I felt slightly feeble at the knees. 'You're sure? You're absolutely, one hundred per cent sure?'

Izzy shrugged. 'Well, I saw him open a drawer and take a pen out, but apart from that, no, he hasn't budged.'

Black Suit Man slotted his phone back into his top pocket. Then he walked out of the restaurant again.

I sat gazing at the getting-a-bit-cold-but-really-nice-looking tomato soup in front of me. I dug out my notebook.

Was I going mad, or had I just witnessed the impossible? Time: seven thirty-eight p.m.

A Page From My Notebook

Think! Think! Any ideas?

There are two Bryan Beekses! Not very likely. A clone suddenly turns up out of the blue? Or a long-lost twin? No, I don't think so.

I really am going loopy! Hmm, yes, that's possible.

I'm mistaken! I haven't really seen what I THINK I've seen. Yes, logically that's probably it. But how?

Is Beeks acting alone? Does he have help? If so, who? (Am I any nearer to discovering the identity of the mysterious texter? Er, no. It could still be anyone! Probably someone in this hotel . . .)

Three urgent questions:
- HAS Beeks stolen the diamonds?
- WHAT can I do when Moss finds out?
- HAVE I totally failed?

CHAPTER
FIVE

MY NOTEBOOK SCRIBBLING WAS INTERRUPTED by a second crashing sound coming from reception. Several more diners gave another small cheer.

A plate of delicious-smelling curry and rice was placed in front of me by Vernon the waiter, along with a naan and a tiny pot of chutney. He took away my bowl of barely-touched-but-very-tasty tomato soup with a sniff.

Finally taking note of Black Suit Man's absence again, I began to put two and two together, made three, added one, and arrived at the correct answer. An important element of the evening's events was at last becoming clear to me!

I had a quick go at the curry. It tasted even better than it looked, but there was no time for that now. I told Izzy to watch Beeks like a hawk and I hurried back to reception.

As I expected, there was Black Suit Man. He had an armful of leaflets and Susan's mum was, once again, putting the display stand back into place.

'I'm so, *so* sorry!' declared Black Suit Man. 'Trust me to forget that map and then knock the whole thing over *again*. I'm being a total pain in the neck tonight. I do apologise.'

'No problem, sir,' said Susan's mum, with a look on her face which said, 'Yes, you *are* being a total pain in the neck'. She slotted the last few leaflets back into the stand. 'Right now, sir, do you have your map?'

'Yes!' said Black Suit Man, waving a leaflet. 'I'm going back to the restaurant, and I promise I won't come near this stand again!'

'Not a problem, sir, really,' said Susan's mum, in a tone of voice which said, 'Yes, it's a huge problem and if you knock this stand over one more time I've going to knock *you* flat on your face'.

Black Suit Man sauntered casually back in the direction of La Splendide. I scooted over to the reception desk.

'Honestly,' growled Susan's mum under her breath. 'Some people!' The faint sound of Bryan Beeks tapping at his laptop came from inside the office. The *Do Not Disturb* sign was still hanging a bit off-centre.

I smiled to myself. This whole weird evening was rapidly sorting itself out in my mind.

It's here that you need to cast your mind back to that

magician I told you about. The one on TV who fooled me for a while into thinking he'd predicted those lottery numbers. I remembered how I'd worked that one out – how the magician had done some very simple things, but in a very roundabout way, to produce an apparently impossible result.

I had no doubt. Beeks had stolen those diamonds. He'd stolen the diamonds *and* he'd never left that office. In a simple, but roudabout sort of way.

What finally made me so sure was spotting the answer to an important question: Where had he hidden the gems? The solution to that little problem convinced me that I was right and that the theft had indeed taken place.

It was all down to one small detail. I'd encountered Mr Beeks twice since arriving at the hotel and there had been one difference, one physical change, between our first meeting and our second. Something to do with that phoney leg injury of his.

Can you spot it too?

The first time I met him, in the admin office, I'd noticed how light that walking stick of his had been. When I bumped into him upstairs, and handed the same walking stick back to him, it had been heavier.

Why the difference in weight? It must have been hollow. There must now be something hidden inside it.

The diamonds.

I looked at my watch – the time was exactly seven forty-eight p.m. I ran back to the restaurant's entrance. Black Suit Man was now nibbling at a salad. Moss the smuggler was wading through a giant plateful of steak and chips. Susan, Izzy and the other girls were tucking into their main courses and nattering away to each other.

I caught Izzy's eye and beckoned to her urgently. She pulled a face at me. I beckoned even more urgently and eventually she came over.

'What?' she said.

'Have you been watching Beeks in that office?'

'Yeeeees,' she sighed. 'And no, he hasn't budged.'

'I bet he closed the blinds a couple of minutes ago,' I said.

Izzy gaped at me. 'Yes! How did you know?'

'It happened earlier. It confirms what I've already suspected. You and the others have to come to the admin office with me. Now. Beeks has nicked those diamonds and we have to stop him.'

'He can't have. He's been in that office all the time,' said Izzy.

'Get the others and come with me. Now!'

'We're in the middle of dinner!'

'Well, get them to do you doggy bags! This is urgent! And be subtle! Don't draw attention to yourselves! The smuggler, over there, and that guy in the black suit, over there, must *not* suspect we know the truth!'

Izzy hurried back to Susan's table. She spoke to them for a minute or two. They all gasped loudly and stared at me. With a hurried shifting of chairs and a burst of excited chatter, they jumped up and raced across the room. Everyone in the restaurant watched them go, including Moss and Black Suit Man.

'I said *don't* draw attention!' I hissed.

'This is really great!' giggled Susan. 'Diamond smugglers! And on my birthday!'

'Shhhhhh!' I said. 'I've told you before, this is not a game! If I didn't need witnesses, I'd . . . Oh, never mind, come on.'

I led them back to reception.

Susan's mum wasn't exactly keen on the idea of us all going into the office and confronting Bryan Beeks. She was even less keen on the idea of her coming in there with us.

'But this is important!' I protested. 'If I'm right, we'll

be preventing a major crime! No, two major crimes, because we'll have got a shipment of stolen diamonds back from those smugglers as well!'

'And if you're wrong?' said Susan's mum.

'I'm not wrong,' I said, hoping to goodness that I wasn't wrong.

I opened the door of the admin office. There was Mr Beeks, sitting at the nearest desk exactly as expected.

'Sorry to disturb you, Bryan,' said Susan's mum, 'but Saxby here thinks you've nicked a load of diamonds.'

Mr Beeks laughed heartily. 'Really? That's interesting! I've never been a desperate criminal on the run before. When did I make off with the loot, then?'

'About twenty minutes ago,' I said.

He laughed again. 'Wow! And how did I do that, then, when I haven't left this office for over an hour?'

'That's true,' said Susan. 'We could all see him from the restaurant. He was in here all that time.'

'Ah,' said Beeks, 'looks like you've spotted the fatal flaw in your friend's argument, Susan. I have a perfect alibi.'

'Yes, rather too perfect,' I said. 'You're in here, with orders not to be disturbed, guarded by Susan's mum on the desk out there and clearly seen by every last person in the restaurant across the courtyard. An absolutely, totally, one hundred per cent watertight alibi.'

'I'm afraid so,' chuckled Mr Beeks. 'Now, if you don't mind, I've still got work to do. You kids run along and play your games somewhere else, eh?'

'One hundred per cent watertight,' I said, 'thanks to *that*.' I pointed up to the projector attached to the ceiling, the one I'd noticed when I'd first visited the office, the one that was just like the equipment at school.

'I think the sequence of events went like this,' I said. 'A while ago, you planned to rob the diamond smuggler you knew would be in the hotel this evening. You knew you'd need an iron-clad alibi to escape suspicion when the smugglers started looking for who'd stolen from them. So last time you were in this office, you recorded a video of yourself working at that desk, including the sounds you made typing at your laptop.

'Tonight, you put a *Do Not Disturb* sign on the door. You sat working at the desk for a short while. Then you got up and closed the blinds. I saw you do that from where I was sitting in the restaurant. In the thirty seconds this room was hidden from view, you turned the projector so that it was facing the window. You set up a screen of some sort, linked your laptop to the projector and started showing the video you'd taken of yourself. You even thought to reverse the image so that it would appear normal from the other side.

'You opened the blinds. From across the courtyard,

nothing appeared to have changed. Except that we were watching the video, not the real Bryan Beeks. You were now free to leave the office with your alibi in place. However, you still needed to get past Susan's mum and anyone else who happened to be in the reception area. If someone saw you leaving the office, your alibi would be useless. And this is where you needed an accomplice, a helper.'

Beeks laughed softly to himself. 'You've got imagination, kid, I'll give you that.'

Everyone else was looking back and forth between me and Beeks. Except for Susan's mum, who was looking straight at me with an expression which said, 'Yes, you really are as strange as I first thought.'

'Your accomplice,' I continued, 'is currently in the restaurant. He's the man wearing the smart black suit. I still can't for the life of me work out where I know him from. Anyway, he arrived at the hotel at a pre-arranged time, shortly after you'd shut yourself away in here. He waited until the reception area was empty, except for Susan's mum. Then he "accidentally" knocked over the display stand out there. While Susan's mum was busy putting things back, you had a chance to sneak out of the office, unseen by anyone except Black Suit Man.

'You went upstairs, to room 217. I don't yet know how you got into the safe. I can only assume you have some device or other which will read the combination. But in any case, you stole the diamonds.

'You then unexpectedly ran slap bang into me. Your alibi would stick if you'd simply passed someone in a corridor on your way back – they would be unlikely to remember you if asked. But as it was me – someone who knows who you are – things might get awkward. However, you didn't worry too much. It would have been your word against mine and with all those witnesses in the restaurant, the alibi was still pretty safe.

'Of course, you needed to get back into the office. So you called Black Suit Man. I saw him answer his phone when I returned to the restaurant. You told him you were ready to return. So out he went to reception again and, making sure only Susan's mum was around . . . oh what a clumsy clot, he sent that display stand flying again. Susan's mum, really cross this time, was looking the other way when you slipped back to your desk.

'I'd suspected that you'd left this room, because the *Do Not Disturb* sign had been, er, disturbed. That probably wouldn't have happened unless the door had been opened and closed.

'Once you were back in the office, you closed the blinds. You switched off the projector, turned it to face the other way again, put the screen away, and reopened the blinds. And there you were once more, in this office, working away, as if nothing had happened, in full view of everyone in the restaurant. Perfect alibi.'

Beeks laughed and clapped his hands. 'That's ingenious,' he chortled. 'I wish I'd really thought of that.'

'Some very simple things, done in a very roundabout way, to produce an apparently impossible result,' I said.

While I'd been talking, Izzy had been examining the room. At that moment, she reached behind one of the piles of cardboard boxes that littered the room and pulled out a large sheet of thin paper. It was pinned to a narrow wooden frame with small hooks attached at one side.

She turned it over for a few seconds, frowning at it. Then she raised it up and neatly hooked it to the top edge of the office window. The view of the dark courtyard and the brightly lit restaurant beyond was precisely covered up.

Everyone turned to look at Bryan Beeks. Any hint of laughter had drained from his face.

'Just because something is possible,' he said, 'doesn't mean it's true.' He turned to Susan's mum. 'Mel, are you going to let this kid accuse me of robbery?'

For the first time, I couldn't work out what Susan's mum was thinking. 'I'm going to let him have his say,' she muttered.

'You have no proof!' cried Mr Beeks. 'Where are these

diamonds, then, eh?'

'You needed a really good hiding place,' I said, 'in case something went wrong. If the smugglers found out about the robbery too early, anything might happen. You needed to be sure that your alibi would hold up and that the diamonds wouldn't be found on you. If we hadn't come in here now, you would have passed the diamonds to Black Suit Man when – oh, what a coincidence! – you left the office just as he left the restaurant. Black Suit Man would then have walked out of here taking them with him. After that, it wouldn't matter what the smugglers did. They'd have no reason to suspect you and the diamonds would be long gone.'

Beeks snorted and shook his head. 'So where is this hiding place, then?'

I picked up the walking stick that was propped against the desk. The moment I touched it, the expression on Beeks's face changed.

The handle was screwed on tightly. I struggled with it at first, but then it snapped loose, like the top coming off a jar of chutney.

A horrible thought suddenly occurred to me. What if I was too late? What if he'd already moved the diamonds? What if he'd transferred them to some other hiding place? I'd have no proof. None at all – or at least nothing beyond a few coincidences and possibilities.

Beeks would get away with it. I'd look like a total idiot.

With trembling hands, I placed the handle of the walking stick on the desk. I tipped up the long, tubular section.

I tipped it some more. Nothing was coming out. I got a cold, creeping feeling down my spine.

With a sudden rush, a glittering flow of light dropped out on to the desk in front of me. There must have been several dozen diamonds, all of them sparkling brightly in the glow from the overhead lighting.

Susan and the others wow-ed and hey-ed and holy-cow-ed. Izzy's face was a mask of astonishment.

'Bryan,' said Susan's mum quietly, 'I think you'd better stay right where you are. Girls, don't let him leave this room.' Susan and her friends blocked the doorway, arms crossed.

'We need to stop Black Suit Man,' I said, 'before he leaves the hotel. We may never trace him if he gets away.'

'I'll go and have a word with Vernon and Susan's dad,' she said. 'We'll find a way to keep him here until the police arrive.'

'Don't alert him,' I said. 'And don't alert Mr Moss, the smuggler, either. There's an entire organisation behind that guy. We must leave him to the cops – it could get dangerous.'

Susan's mum gave me a nod and disappeared. I turned to Mr Beeks as I rummaged in my pocket for my phone.

'How did you open the safe?' I said.

Beeks reached over and picked up the handle of his walking stick. He clicked a tiny catch at its end and opened it up into two halves. Inside was a device which looked a bit like a small pen.

He took it out and placed it on the desk. Then, with a violent crunch, he smashed down on it with his fist. Izzy and the others flinched. He swept the broken bits in to the waste paper basket.

'Temper temper,' I mumbled.

Now that the case was concluded, I turned my attention to the mysterious texter. I switched on my phone and sent him/her a brief message:

Robbery foiled. Diamonds in my possession. Police being called.

I pressed *Send*. Ha! Whoever the texter was, he/she would be hugely impressed with me. They'd also be shaking in their boots, because they'd realise that if I could wrap up this case so efficiently, then I'd be hot on their heels and discover their identity before you could ——

BEEP. A-ha, an answer. Congratulations, no doubt!

I leaned over to Susan. 'Er, I don't suppose the restaurant could warm up that curry for me? I'm starving.'

Then I held up my phone,

No!!! Told you to prevent robbery only! Told you not to interfere! Smugglers' meeting MUST take place at 9 p.m. Codename Heather is NOT a smuggler, is an UNDERCOVER MI5 AGENT. Heather will arrest Moss when sees Moss has diamonds. Moss MUST not suspect. Entire MI5 operation at stake, months of investigation.

Oh dear.

Remember that cold, creeping feeling I got down my spine when I opened the walking stick? I got it again.

The time was eight twelve p.m.

CHAPTER SIX

'OH NOOOOO!' I WAILED.

'What's the matter?' said Izzy.

'Arrghh! Why didn't Mr Bloomin' Mystery bloomin' well *tell me*?' I cried.

'Tell you what?' said Izzy.

For a second or two, I was so frozen with terror and indecision that I think I could hear my brain ticking. Then I hurriedly gathered up the diamonds.

'We've got to move quickly! It's . . . eight thirteen p.m. We have forty-seven minutes, maximum.'

'To do what?' said Izzy.

I ushered her out into the reception area, leaving Susan and the other girls to keep watch on Beeks.

'To get these diamonds back into the safe in room 217,

without Moss the smuggler knowing about it and before his contact turns up.'

'Why?' said Izzy.

I told her. She nearly went 'Arrghh!' too.

'We need Muddy,' I said, finding his number on my phone. My conversation with Muddy went like this:

Me: Muddy! Can you open a locked safe?

Muddy: Hmmm. What sort of safe?

Me: Number combination, the kind you reset, like you find in hotel rooms.

Muddy: Hmmm. Not sure. Let me go and see what I've got in my Development Laboratory. Hang on.

Me: No, wait! We can't wait while you root around in your garage! Yes or no? Quick!

Muddy: Then yes. Well . . . probably.

Me: Great! Get over here now! I'm at the Regal Hotel!

Muddy: Forget it, matey, you're on your own.

Me: WHAT?

Muddy: I'm not turning up to Susan Lillington's girlie sleepover! If one of those girls has locked her make-up or something in a safe, you can deal with it on your own.

Me: Forget the sleepover! This is urgent! I'm on a case!

Muddy: Nope. You got yourself into it, you can get yourself out.

I squeezed my eyes tightly shut. I was going to have to tell him the truth. He would go bananas.

Me: Please?

Muddy: Nope. You won't get me within a mile of that girlie sleepover, and that's my final word.

Me (deep breath): MI5 is involved. Truly. I'm not joking.

Silence.

Muddy: I'll be there in ten minutes.

Nine minutes and forty-two seconds later, he came hurtling into the hotel, gasping for breath, with a large grubby bag of assorted gadgets slung over his shoulder.

'Where are they?' he said. If his eyes had been any gogglier they'd have dropped out of his head. He scampered about like a puppy that's been promised a new squeaky toy.

'On their way,' I said. 'In the meantime, we have work to do. Well, *you* have work to do.'

The time was eight twenty-four p.m. Susan's mum reappeared from the direction of the restaurant.

'Sorted,' she said. 'Vernon's accidentally on purpose spilled gravy down Black Suit Man's trousers. They've got him in the kitchens, apologising and soaking out the stain.'

'Brilliant,' I said. 'Izzy, keep an eye out for Moss the smuggler. We have to be finished before he returns to his room. He'll go back upstairs as soon as he's polished off that gigantic free dinner. Call us the moment he passes through here.'

Muddy and I raced for the stairs. Then we raced back again. Susan's mum handed us a duplicate keycard for room 217. *Then* we raced for the stairs.

Two minutes later, we were in the smuggler's lair! The curtains had been drawn and a briefcase had been dropped on to the bed.

I opened the wardrobe. The squat metal hatch of the room safe was firmly shut.

'Why couldn't Beeks have left it open?' I muttered to myself.

'Good thing he didn't,' said Muddy cheerily, 'otherwise you wouldn't have needed me.' He pulled a couple of electronic gizmos out of his bag. He clipped one end of the first gizmo to the safe and listened carefully to the other as he made delicate adjustments.

'Spies!' he giggled happily. 'Real spies! Just like I've always wanted!'

'Yeah, OK, calm down,' I muttered. 'You and Susan seem to be finding this case highly entertaining.'

'I always told you to be more spyish,' said Muddy, turning dials on a homemade oddity he'd constructed out of an old pocket calculator. 'Haven't I always told you to be more spyish?'

'Detective work is nothing like being a spy,' I insisted. 'I am not a spy. You are not a spy.'

'Sooooo, we're doing something a spy would do and

there's a spy coming here soon, doing undercover stuff like spies do . . . but we're not spies.'

'No. It's just this one time, OK?'

'If you say so.' Muddy grinned. 'You see this lock-picking gear I'm using?'

'Yes?'

'I bet spies use stuff like that.'

'Oh, get on with it. I wish I'd never told you.'

The time was eight thirty-six p.m. Moss the smuggler could arrive at any moment.

Muddy listened as the machine beside the safe click-bleep-blipped. He switched it off and slung it back into his bag.

'No good, I'll try something else.'

The seconds ticked away. I glanced around. The room felt gloomy and cold. I closed my fists to stop my hands shaking. My heart was pattering like a drum roll.

Why did I get myself into this? Exactly how much trouble would we be in if this all went wrong?

CLUNK!

'Done it!' cried Muddy. The safe's door swung open.

My phone warbled. It was Izzy.

'Get out of there!' she said. 'Moss has just passed us. He'll be at his room in seconds!'

Sitting inside the safe was a little black drawstring bag. Fumbling awkwardly, my pulse beating against the sides of my head, I took the bag and filled it with the diamonds from my pocket.

'Shall we keep one?' whispered Muddy.

'*No!*'

'Just one?'

'*No!*'

I kept glancing at the thin bar of light that showed under the door of the room. We wouldn't hear Moss approaching, not with those thick carpets everywhere. I slipped the bag back into the safe and closed it up again.

'C'mon, move!'

We scurried out of the room, taking care to make sure the door was shut behind us. We walked as calmly as our screaming nerves would allow.

We passed Moss on the stairs. He didn't give us so much as a second glance. We tried not to stare at him with raw fear in our eyes. He patted his chest and burped quietly to himself.

'That was close,' whispered Muddy, as we arrived at reception.

'The police are on their way,' said Susan's mum. Several of Susan's friends were still in the admin office, keeping guard on Mr Beeks. The rest of us zipped across the reception area and sat on the wide leather sofas that were next to the leaflet display stand.

We tried to look casual, as if we were simply lounging about without a care in the world. I don't think we succeeded very well. Most of us were looking around like a bunch of meerkats on red alert. Izzy tried playing a game on her phone and kept dropping it. Muddy had picked up a magazine from the coffee table beside the sofas and was reading it upside down. The magazine was upside down, I mean, not Muddy.

Minutes passed. Every second felt like a hundred million years. A couple of hotel guests checked in and a couple of hotel guests went out and diners came and went from the restaurant.

Eight fifty p.m. I felt a shock of cold air as the glass entrance door swung open. I turned to see a tall, angular woman crossing the lobby. She had a beautifully sculptured face and long, brown hair. Her sharply tailored outfit had narrow lapels at the neck and her broad trousers flapped around her high-heeled shoes. She went over to the reception desk.

'Hello,' she said to Susan's mum. 'I believe I'm expected by a Mr Moss you have staying here? My name is Heather.'

I suddenly noticed that Muddy was staring at her. I couldn't recall the last time I'd seen someone gape so open-mouthed at anything.

He nudged me in the ribs as 'Heather' headed for the

stairs and out of sight. 'Now that's what I call a spy,' he breathed. 'I think I'm in love.'

A lot happened in the next five minutes. The police arrived. Some of them piled into the admin office to collar Beeks, some of them hurried towards the restaurant to collar Black Suit Man. 'Heather' reappeared, frog-marching a handcuffed Moss in front of her.

All three villains (Black Suit Man with gravy stains all down his legs) were escorted out of the hotel, past where I, Muddy, Izzy, Susan and the other girls were still perched on the sofas. The villains were bundled out into the freezing night air, towards a flashing shimmer of police car lights which glinted off the snow.

As if a switch had been thrown, the girls all started chattering at once. They agreed that this was definitely the best birthday sleepover any of them had ever been to, ever. With a flurry of 'Bye's and 'See ya, guys's they went up to their room. Susan's mum stood behind the reception desk with a look on her face which said, 'Yes, this is definitely the weirdest evening I've ever had, ever'.

Muddy slung his bag of gizmos over his shoulder. 'Bye, Saxby,' he said, still a bit awestruck by the memory of Heather, or whatever her real name might have been. 'An actual spy. I don't think I can ever thank you enough.'

By now, I was feeling as crumpled and worn out as a pre-owned tissue. I was about to head home myself, when I caught sight of a short figure wrapped in an overcoat, lurking beside the leaflet stand.

It was Inspector Godalming, he of the whistling false teeth and the birdish walk. I walked across the lobby to him, shaking my head slowly, hand slapped to my forehead.

Remember that one and only vague clue I had to the identity of the mysterious texter? It hadn't been *what* he'd said, so much as the fact that he'd said it at all. The texter had to be someone in the know, someone who had *access* to the kind of information he'd given me. (And as soon as he'd told me that 'Heather' was from MI5, I'd realised that my initial fears were unfounded and that the texter was one of the good guys after all – the smugglers would have wanted to make sure MI5's plan went wrong.)

'It was you, wasn't it?' I said. 'You sent me those texts.'

'Yesh, I'm afraid sho, shonny,' said Inspector Godalming. (We'll take the badly-fitting dentures as read from now on, otherwise it's a bit of a spelling nightmare!) 'I thought you might have known it was me once you saw Sergeant Willis.'

'Who?' I said.

139

'The man in the black suit?'

'He was a police officer? Of course! *That's* where I'd seen him before! With you. He was there when you arrested Elsa Moreaux. Argh, I should have realised!' I thought for a moment. 'And that's why you called on me. You knew a police officer was mixed up with Beeks's scheme to steal the diamonds. So I take it you didn't know *which* police officer?'

'Correct,' said the Inspector. 'And that's *one* reason I called on you. Beeks has been in trouble before, but there was no way he could have known about the diamonds unless someone under my command had told him about them. As I had no idea who that was, any enquiries at the police station ran a high risk of alerting the guilty officer to the fact that they were being investigated and that someone at the hotel had learned of Beeks's plan.'

'So who *was* your source of information inside the hotel?' I said.

'The restaurant's head waiter,' said the Inspector.

'Vernon. You know, I barely even considered it was him!' (Did *you*?) 'But why was it *me* you contacted? You've always gone on about how much you disapprove of me "interfering in police work"!'

'Yes, well,' muttered Inspector Godalming, bristling with embarrassment like a parrot flapping on its perch.

'I would have used a grown-up private eye, but if a member of my own squad was a bad apple, I couldn't be sure that any investigator wasn't one too. And in any case, I knew young Susan's father from his days in the police force. I know she goes to the same school as you, so I knew you'd have no difficulty being here without raising Beeks's suspicions.'

'I see,' I said. 'Which only leaves the MI5 connection . . .'

'The security services had been tracking those smugglers for months,' said the Inspector. 'This meeting tonight was their one and only chance to catch Moss red-handed. They contacted us, told us what was going on and warned us that nothing, absolutely nothing, must get in the way of them arresting him. There couldn't be the faintest whiff of a cop within five miles of this place tonight, not until Moss was captured. We even had to delay responding to Susan's mother's call until we got the nod.'

'But your bad apple, Sergeant Willis, threw a spanner in the works,' I said. 'He told Beeks about the diamonds, Beeks devised the robbery and the pair of them were set to walk off with the gems.'

'Correct,' said the Inspector. 'When I found out, through Vernon, I was in a right panic. I couldn't be seen to interfere with tonight's events, or MI5 would come down on us like a ton of bricks. But I also couldn't risk

Beeks succeeding, or MI5 would *still* have come down on us like a ton of bricks.'

'So you texted me,' I said, 'and kept your identity secret from me until it was all over.'

'Couldn't risk you blabbering something at the wrong moment now, could I, sonny? You nearly blew the entire operation as it was!'

'Er, yes, well,' I mumbled. Now it was my turn to feel embarrassed. 'No harm done, eh? All's well that ends well.'

I turned to go.

'Needless to say, sonny,' said Inspector Godalming, his shoulders twitching inside his overcoat, 'none of this ever happened. Officially. Right?'

I grinned. 'As ever. Can't have brilliant schoolboy detectives interfering with police work, can we?'

I had a long and icy walk home, but something kept me smiling all the way.

Case closed.

CASE FILE TWENTY-FOUR:

THE GUY
WHO CAME IN
FROM THE COLD

CHAPTER ONE

I HAVE A VERY LOUD SNEEZE. I can't help it.

I have a sneeze which makes people leap up, yelping, as if a major environmental disaster had suddenly started shaking the building. I don't mean to make people jump. I just do. That's just how my nose is.

I was making everyone jump at school one Tuesday morning. I was feeling dreadful. All that sitting around in my shed in the freezing weather (and all that tramping about in the snow on the trail of assorted bad guys) had finally caught up with me. I had officially got the World's Snottiest Cold. By lunchtime, our form tutor Mrs Penzler had had enough.

'Saxby,' she cried, pulling her shoulders back and covering her ears, 'I could hear you sneezing all the way from the main hall!'

'Sorry, Mrs Penzler,' I said. Although, with my thickly bunged-up sinuses, what I actually said was, 'Sobby, Bisses Benzlub.'

'Why don't you go home, Saxby?' she said. Mrs Penzler doesn't really *do* sympathy, so this was more like a direct order. 'Come back to school when you're better.'

'Yedd, Bisses Benzlub. *WHA-CHOOOOO!*'

The entire class jumped. I think the floor may have wobbled too.

By the time I got home, I was feeling even worse. I had some chicken soup. I don't know why. People are always offering you chicken soup when you're ill, so it seemed like the thing to do.

I went to bed. Crawled to bed, to be honest.

The window in my room is quite high off the floor. So as I lay there, all I could see outside was a dull, blank rectangle of sky. There wasn't a sound coming from anywhere and I had that peculiar, cut-off feeling you get when you're at home on a school day. You know the feeling I mean?

I spent the rest of the day snuggled up in bed, reading a very interesting book about real-life police investigations. Partly, this was research for the Detective Handbook I keep meaning to write, but mostly it was because I was too bunged-up and sneezy to sleep.

Anyway, this book had some fascinating things to say about *witnesses* to crimes. All too often, said the book, witnesses may not even realise they *are* witnesses. It may be that nobody knows the importance of something they've seen or heard. It's only when a detective comes along, gathers up all the evidence, and notices connections, that the complete picture can be seen.

As it turned out, this observation was to be hugely important over the next few days. A new case file was about to come to my attention. As case files go, it was quite a small and easy-to-solve one, but it's worth telling you about because it's a good example of how an entire problem can be sorted out with the help of a reliable witness or two.

What I didn't realise, lying there sneezing, was that I'd have to solve this particular puzzle without moving from my bed.

CHAPTER
TWO

'*WHA-CHOOOOO!*

'What the —'

'*WHA-CHOOOOOOOO!* Sorry.'

'I think I've gone deaf.'

My great friend Isobel 'Izzy' Moustique, our school's Number One Boffin, sat at the far end of my bed. At arm's length, she held out some more paper tissues for me.

'Thanks,' I said.

'Catch it, bin it, kill it,' she muttered. 'And in your case, Saxby, put a sock in it as well.'

'Sorry,' I mumbled, recoiling slightly at what my nose had just left on the tissues.

'You're not feeling any better then?' Izzy asked.

'No, I feel lousy,' I grumbled. 'I've finished reading my book, the telly's broken and there's no more chicken soup. Have you brought me anything?'

She raised a finger. 'Yes, I have.'

From the self-decorated canvas bag that rested beside her ankles, she drew out a large paper file.

'Homework,' she said, handing it over. 'When Mrs Penzler heard I was coming over to see you tonight, she gave me this to give to you.'

'Oh. How kind. Thank you enormously,' I said. Can you detect the tiny little hint of grumpy sarcasm in my voice?

'It's not my fault,' said Izzy. 'Mrs Penzler's been in a mood all day.'

'She's in a mood most days,' I said.

'No, I mean a *real* mood,' said Izzy. 'Extra maths tests, the lot.'

'Why?'

Izzy started to fiddle with the chunky rings that dotted her fingers. She'd obviously been home before coming to see me because she was wearing her usual out-of-school mixture of bright colours and flared cuffs. I wondered why she hadn't come straight from school.

'Oh, it's . . . I dunno, just one of her moods,' she said.

'No, it isn't. I can tell,' I persisted. 'What's happened?'

Izzy squidged her face around a bit before replying.

'There's a book gone missing. It's one Mrs Penzler brought from home.'

'What sort of book?' I said, wiping my nose with another tissue.

'Yesterday, after you went home,' said Izzy, 'we started a new history topic. We're doing British Society and Culture after World War II. And before you say anything, some of it looks like it's going to be quite interesting.'

'Does it include crime?'

'No.'

'I see. Carry on.'

'So. New topic. Mrs Penzler produced this slightly tatty old book. It's a school English textbook from about sixty years ago, which belonged to her father. It turns out she comes from a long line of teachers.'

'Poor woman,' I mumbled. Mrs Penzler was as tough as a school carrot, so it wasn't often anyone ever said that about her. 'It's sixty years old and it belonged to her dad? How old *is* she, exactly?'

'Oooh, about two hundred and forty?' said Izzy. 'She said it's her most treasured possession.'

'A school textbook? Poor woman.'

'Stop interrupting,' said Izzy. 'She said this textbook would be good background information for us. It would give us an idea of the sort of things that were studied at school all those years ago. She left it on the row of shelves beside the door and said we could take a look at it whenever we liked, so long as it didn't leave the classroom, OK. One or two of us had a look before we went home yesterday and I saw a couple more taking a look first thing this morning before registration. Then, late this afternoon, Mrs Penzler asked where it was. Nobody knew. It wasn't on the shelf. "Who's got it?" she said. No hands up, nothing. And she blew her top.'

'And out comes the extra homework,' I said.

'Exactly,' said Izzy. 'It's put everyone on edge. Mrs Penzler can be a bit of a grouch, but it's not as if we all *dislike* her or anything. None of us would *steal* something of hers. She started going on about how she can't trust her own class any more, and how sad it was that one of us could take something she values so much. She got quite teary.'

'Mrs Penzler?' I gasped.

'Yes, Mrs Penzler! The whole class is feeling sorry for her one minute and glaring suspiciously at each other the next. I dread to think what things are going to be like in that classroom tomorrow. You're well out of it. *And* you'll miss the Winter Fayre tomorrow, you lucky —'

'Wooo-hoo! I'd forgotten about the Winter Fayre,' I said. 'Missing that is the best news I've had all term.'

The St Egbert's School Winter Fayre was an annual

torture which took place on the coldest, darkest, most miserable day of the entire school year. Pupils, teachers, parents and other family members would cram into the main hall after lessons. They would shuffle from one feeble stall to another, buying assorted tat and revolting-looking homemade cakes. Everyone would get jostled, bad tempered and boiling hot in their winter coats. Then the next day, the Head would declare what a marvellous success it had been and how it had raised a record amount of cash for school funds.

'Could you cough on me a bit,' said Izzy, 'so I'll have an excuse to miss it too?'

'Tell me about this textbook first,' I said. 'I assume it's a valuable item, being so old?'

'No, just the opposite,' said Izzy. 'That's the mystery. It's worthless. You might as well steal a toilet roll. It has huge sentimental value for Mrs Penzler, but that's it.'

'Hmmm,' I said. 'That's odd. Describe it.'

'It's a small, pale green hardback. Quite tatty, battered at the edges. It's about three centimetres thick, about ten centimetres wide and about twenty centimetres high.'

'Not a large object, then?' I said.

'No,' Izzy said, shrugging. 'Pretty standard book size.'

'And who knew it was there, on the shelf?'

'Only Mrs Penzler and our class. Nobody else. That's why she's sure one of us took it.'

'Nobody could have seen it there and thought it was worth nicking?'

'I doubt it,' said Izzy. 'Like I said, it's a tatty old thing.'

'Has anything else happened today?' I said. 'Anything unusual been going on?'

'Actually, yes,' said Izzy. 'Bob Thompson's been acting weird, but that's nothing to do with the book.'

'Weird? How?'

'Well, sort of . . . helpful, pleasant. Rather creepy, really.'

'Bob Thompson? Being nice? Eurgh, yeah, gives you the shudders.'

Bob Thompson was the school's premier league bully. He looked like a walking block of concrete with a head poking out of the top – the sort of person you'd expect to see chewing on broken bottles and new-born kittens. Luckily, his class was at the other end of the school. (For more information on Bob Thompson, see my earlier case file, *The Hangman's Lair*.)

'Why's he being nice?' I asked.

'I guess the Head's threatening him with permanent exclusion again,' said Izzy. 'He's been running errands for teachers and helping out with the Winter Fayre. But that's the only other unusual thing that's been going on.'

'Hmmm,' I said. 'Well, if Bob Thompson has been volunteering for the Winter Fayre, that's one more reason not to go!'

'I'd better be getting home,' said Izzy. 'Extra homework to do, don't forget.'

She stood up to go, then paused. From her bag, she produced a jumbo-sized bar of chocolate. She placed it on the bed beside me.

'You didn't really think I wouldn't bring you anything, did you?' She grinned. 'I could tell you were wondering why I'd been home before coming over. I didn't want that thing melting in my bag all day, did I?'

I smiled and blew my nose.

A Page From My Notebook

(Page slightly illegible as dabbed in chocolatey
fingermarks, ahem, ahem.)

FACT 1: The missing book is not large.

FACT 2: The missing book is not worth anything very
much.

FACT 3: The missing book is . . . er, missing.

Some observations:

Fact 1 means it could easily be slipped into a school bag.
In theory, ANYONE in the class could have taken it.

BUT! As Izzy said, why steal it? Nobody appears to have
a MOTIVE, a reason for nicking the thing. Fact 2 would
seem to rule that out.

If money isn't a motive, could it be that someone is
simply out to upset Mrs Penzler? BUT! As Izzy also said,
would anyone in our class want to be that cruel? It
doesn't seem likely.

Bob Thompson would be that cruel. No question. BUT! He
wouldn't steal the book and he wouldn't thump someone

into stealing it for him. Why? He didn't even know it was there! And if he HAD known about it, he'd also have known it was worthless, so he STILL wouldn't have nicked it.

There is one other possible explanation for the theft: that whoever took it THOUGHT, wrongly, that it WAS valuable. Should that be the line of enquiry I pursue?

CHAPTER
THREE

THE MYSTERY OF THE MISSING book preyed on my mind that night. I still couldn't get to sleep, what with the coughing and the sneezing and the *WHA-CHOOOOOO*-ing. The problem swirled around inside my head like an irritating tune you can't stop humming.

At about eleven on Thursday morning, I texted my other great friend, George 'Muddy' Whitehouse, St Egbert's School's leading inventor of all things gadgety. I needed a detailed account of what had happened in our classroom while I'd been away. I needed a reliable witness!

My text asked him to give some careful thought to the exact sequence of events on Tuesday afternoon and Wednesday. And then to come and see me straight after school. Well, straight after the Winter Fayre, which was straight after school.

'Hi!' I said. 'Have you brought me anything?'

He looked confused. 'No.'

'You've just been shuffling around a school hall full with things to buy – haven't you got me anything at all?'

'I didn't get anything for *you*, you cheeky —'

'What did you get then?' I asked.

'Wrapping paper, cards, birthday pressies for my aunties and three boxes of sponge cake with icing on top. And my mother doesn't like any of them.'

'Wasn't she there?' I said.

'No, she stayed in the car,' grumbled Muddy. 'Said she couldn't face the Winter Fayre again. Gave me a list. I told her if she didn't like the cakes I chose, hard luck. That's what you get for being a yellow-bellied chicken!'

'Was it really bad this year?' I murmured, afraid.

'Worse than ever,' shuddered Muddy. 'Packed out. I thought I was going to be trampled in the rush for the Pre-owned Uniform stall. I've been developing a personal electric shock zapper in my laboratory, the Whitehouse Buzz-U-Back Mark II, and I very nearly used it. The teachers swiped most of the chocolate cake. You'd think they get enough of it in the staff room, but no . . .'

'Yeah, yeah, shut up. Have you done what I told you

to do in my text? Have you given some careful thought to Tuesday and Wednesday?'

'Yes.'

'Good.'

'Is that lemon squash you've got there?' he said, pointing to the glass on my bedside cabinet. 'Can I have some?'

'That's to soothe my poor sore throat,' I protested.

'Thanks,' said Muddy and glugged back two thirds of it. 'I'm boiled. You could have roasted a monkey in that hall. And there's bloomin' Bob Thompson barging his way out at the end, kicking little kids. Anyway, right, Tuesday and Wednesday.' He took a deep breath and closed his eyes. 'I am ready. What do you want to know?'

'I want to know about Bob Thompson. He kicked kids out of the way?'

'No, that was just now. Not Tuesday or Wednesday. I thought you wanted to know about Tuesday and Wednesday?' said Muddy.

'Bob Thompson first,' I said. 'He kicked kids?'

Muddy looked puzzled. 'He always does that. That's what he does.'

'Not according to Izzy. Not for the last few days, anyway,' I said.

'Oh, yeah, I know,' said Muddy. 'He has been acting weird. Sort of . . . nice. Eurgh, creepy.'

'But obviously he's back to normal now,' I said.

'Obviously. Did Izzy tell you he helped set the Fayre up? He was still being nice all the way through it, too. He kept carrying stuff out to the car park for people. Must have got too much for him. All that politeness made him snap. He even grunted at the Head.'

Suddenly, my mind was racing fast enough to win a Formula One Grand Prix. Izzy had suggested that Bob Thompson was suddenly being nice because he was under threat of exclusion. But if he *wasn't* being nice any more, if he was suddenly happy to go back to grunting rudely at the Head . . .

What was going on?

'Did anything happen at the Winter Fayre?' I said. 'I mean, to Bob Thompson?'

'I thought you wanted to talk about Tuesday and Wednesday?' cried Muddy.

'In a minute! Did anything happen?'

'Not that I saw,' said Muddy. 'Like I said, he was carrying stuff for people. You know what he's like – he was probably expecting a few parents to give him a fiver or something.'

A-ha! A mental light snapped on in my head and shone on an important possibility. What Muddy had just said made perfect sense – Bob Thompson might have been being nice simply because he *wanted* something.

And *if* that was true . . .

There was an interesting deduction to be made here. If Bob's sudden niceness was all about something he wanted, then it was plain to see that something *had* happened at the Winter Fayre. There was a simple reason why Bob was his usual nasty self again.

Can you spot what it was?

'If Bob's gone back to his usual bullying ways,' I muttered to myself, 'then that suggests he doesn't *need* to be nice any more. Which suggests that, at the Winter Fayre, he finally *got* what he wanted.'

Muddy frowned. 'How do you mean? Got what?'

'Whatever it was he was after,' I said. 'And now we have reason to believe he was after something, instead of trying to avoid exclusion, Mrs Penzler's missing book comes back into the picture.'

'Nahhh!' cried Muddy. 'Bob Thompson never knew about it. And even if he did, it's not worth any money. Even he isn't *that* stupid.'

'Yes, I thought the same myself last night,' I told him. 'So perhaps we should examine what happened on Tuesday and Wednesday.'

'Ah, at last,' said Muddy.

'What happened to Bob Thompson, that is. Forget about our class.'

'*What?*' cried Muddy. 'Oh great, so all that thinking I've been doing today, that was for nothing, was it? I've made notes too, y'know.' He pulled a scraggy mound of scrap paper out of his pocket.

'How many times did you see Bob Thompson on Tuesday and Wednesday?'

'Er . . . none.'

'Not outside, at lunchtime? Nowhere? Check back

162

through your notes,' I said.

Muddy checked his notes. 'Oh, yes, once. He turned up in our class shortly after lunchtime yesterday. He said he was there to collect whatever we were donating to the Winter Fayre. Shirts for the pre-owned uniform stall, odds and ends for the bric-a-brac stall, that sort of thing.'

'So he took it all away with him?' I asked.

'No, it had already gone. That short kid from Mr Nailshott's class, Whatsisface, he'd turned up for it just before lunch.'

'So Bob Thompson didn't take anything away with him?'

'No, he just opened the classroom door, said what he'd come for, Mrs Penzler said Whatsisface from Mr Nailshott's class had already been, thank you. Then he looked around for a second, looked thoroughly miffed, and off he went. He barely set foot in the room. Surely that's not a clue? Nothing happened.'

'What might be significant is that he turned up at all, not what did or didn't happen,' I said.

'Huh?' said Muddy. 'Why?'

'Was Mrs Penzler's book still in the classroom when he appeared?'

'No idea.'

'You said this was straight after lunch? Yes?'

'Yes, about ten minutes,' said Muddy.

'And the whole class was there, from the minute the bell rang?'

Muddy looked at his notes. 'Yes.'

'Did anyone leave the room during the afternoon? No, what I mean is, was the room left empty at all?'

'Emily Jenkins had a nosebleed aaaaaat . . .' He turned a page of notes sideways and squinted at it. '. . . Two thirteen p.m.'

'So the room was occupied for the rest of the school day? And Mrs Penzler found that the book had gone shortly before the end of lessons?'

'That's right. Don't you want to hear about Emily Jenkins's nosebleed?'

'No.'

'It was really yukky.'

'I don't care. We can at least be certain about whether the book was still in the room when Bob Thompson turned up.'

Muddy thought for a moment. 'Can we?'

'Yes.'

Have you worked out if it was there or not?

'If the book had gone by the time lessons ended,' I said, 'and the room was occupied all afternoon, then it can't have been there immediately after lunchtime. Anyone who'd picked it up would have been seen. So it wasn't there when Bob appeared.'

'Er, yes, I was just about to say that,' said Muddy. 'Do you mean it was taken during the lunch break?'

'That's definitely the most likely possibility,' I said. 'Definitely.'

'You're wrong,' said Muddy. 'Mrs Penzler was in the classroom all lunchtime. I know she was – she was marking Monday's history essays and she gave them back to us after lunch. She had her sandwiches at her desk.'

'Oh. Bang goes that theory, then. Ah, no, wait. That means we can say for certain that the book had gone *before* lunchtime,' I said. 'Things are getting clearer by the minute! The book was still there first thing?'

'Yes, it was, I saw it when I arrived at school,' said Muddy.

'OK,' I said, wiping my nose with a fresh tissue. 'Tell me exactly who came in and out of that classroom during the morning.'

Muddy scrambled through his notes. Bits of scrunched up paper littered my bed.

'Nine thirty a.m.,' he said, 'Mrs McEwan from the

school office came in to deliver a load of paperwork to Mrs Penzler, put it on Mrs Penzler's desk. Nine fifty a.m., Jeremy Sweetly left to go to the dentist's. Someone went to the loo at nine seven a.m., nine fifty-one a.m., nine fifty-five a.m. . . . Do you need loo breaks?'

'Probably not, skip those.'

'Breaktime, still thick ice and snow outside, we all stayed indoors. Ten thirty a.m, Thingummy from the year below us came to pick up some maths books, staggered out with heavy box from back of the class. Ten forty-five a.m., Jeremy Sweetly returned from the dentist's, kept dribbling. Eleven a.m., the Ginger Kid from the class next door was sent in to ask Mrs Penzler if they could borrow some scissors, left with a handful from the drawers under the window. Eleven forty-seven a.m., Whatsisface from Mr Nailshott's class turns up to collect donations for the Winter Fayre, gathers them from the shelves beside the door. Eleven forty-nine a.m., Mrs McEwan comes in again, asks Mrs Penzler for paperwork back, handed out by mistake, takes huge pile of stuff from desk. When she's gone, Mrs Penzler has a moan about all these interruptions we're having this morning. And that's it up to the lunchtime bell.'

There it was! Right there, for all to see. I knew at once

what had happened to Mrs Penzler's book. I couldn't be one hundred per cent sure, but ninety per cent seemed good enough to me.

Have you spotted it too?

'How could you lot not have spotted it before?' I cried.

'Spotted what?' said Muddy.

'The book got mixed up in the stuff that Whatsisface from Mr Nailshott's class collected up for the Winter Fayre. It went in with the odds and ends for the bric-a-brac stall. The book was on the shelves by the door, Izzy told me yesterday. And you've just told me that the stuff for the Fayre was there too.'

Muddy snorted loudly. 'Nooooo. The book was on a shelf by itself, the Fayre stuff was all up the other end. You'd have to be a right twit to go picking up a tatty old book like Mrs Penzler's, thinking it . . . Actually, I see what you mean.'

'There's an important principle that Sherlock Holmes sticks by in his stories,' I said. 'Whenever you eliminate the impossible, whatever remains, however improbable, must be the truth. We know the book was there first thing in the morning. We know it had gone by lunchtime. Whatsisface from Mr Nailshott's class was the only person who went near those shelves. He must have picked the book up by mistake.'

'So nobody stole it!' cried Muddy.

'No. Somebody bought it at the Winter Fayre.'

'Oh no, it could be anywhere by now!' said Muddy.

'No. Think back to Bob Thompson. He was after something and, at the Winter Fayre, he found it.'

'That can't be right,' said Muddy. 'Think back to the book. It's worthless. And Bob didn't even know about it, anyway.'

'That's the final part of the mystery,' I said. 'That's the problem we need to solve next! Look at your notes. What precisely happened on Tuesday afternoon, when Mrs Penzler showed you all the book for the first time?'

'I don't have notes about that,' said Muddy.

'Why?'

'I wasn't there. Loo break.'

'*What?* Why didn't you tell me?'

'I didn't know it was important, did I?' protested Muddy. 'You've been going on about Bob Thompson!'

'So who *was* there?'

'Er, well, everyone else.'

I phoned Izzy.

CHAPTER FOUR

'DO WE REALLY HAVE TO do this now?' said Izzy, on the phone. 'I was going to go to bed soon. I think I'm getting your cold. A day too late. The Winter Fayre was *awful*.'

'So I hear,' I said. 'I'm feeling a little bit better now.'

Izzy muttered something I couldn't quite catch.

'I'll put you on speaker,' I said.

Once Izzy, Muddy and I could all hear each other, I propped myself up against my pillows. It seemed that Izzy, much to my surprise (and hers), was herself the vital witness who would crack the case.

'What we need here, Izzy,' I said, 'is an exact description of the point during Tuesday afternoon when Mrs Penzler showed the class that book. The point at which Muddy was in the loo. And the most important question we need answering is: Was Bob Thompson anywhere near at the time?'

'Bob Thompson?' said Izzy. 'Why? What's he got to do with this? He isn't even in our class.'

'But did you or anyone else see him that afternoon?' I said.

Izzy went quiet for a minute or two. 'I think he did put his head around the door,' said Izzy.

'I never knew that!' said Muddy.

'He was delivering a message from Mrs McEwan,' said Izzy. 'But I can't remember when that was.'

I turned to Muddy. 'You missed Bob Thompson *and* Mrs Penzler talking about the book? How long were you in the loo for?'

Muddy went red in the face. 'I got up late. I didn't have time to go before I left home.'

'Never mind,' I said. 'At least now we know Bob appeared while you were in the toilet, which was also when Mrs Penzler showed the class the book.'

'Hang on,' said Izzy. 'I can't be sure about exactly when he appeared. It might have been before Mrs Penzler showed us the book, or it might have been later on. I honestly can't remember.'

'OK,' I said, 'just run through what Mrs Penzler did. As exactly as you can.'

Izzy let out a slow breath. 'Er, right . . . Mrs Penzler

was talking about the new history topic. She said we'd be doing stuff about the 1950s . . . and, lemme think, the moon landings . . .'

'What were her exact words?' I asked.

'Good grief, I can't remember that!' said Izzy. 'Well, not accurately.'

'Approximately, then,' I said. 'As close as you can. Skip to when she showed you the book.'

'She opened the drawer of her desk,' said Izzy. 'She took out the book and she walked around the desk to stand in front of us. She held the book up in one hand. She said . . . it was something like . . . I just can't recall the first bit, but she said something like, "This belonged to my father, who was also a teacher. He taught at a school in Dorset, on the south coast. His father was a teacher, and his father before him. The book has no value in itself, none at all, but it's very precious to me. In fact, it's my most treasured possession. I'm going to leave it on the shelf over there. You're all free to take a look through it, but do please be careful with it. It will give you a feel for what lessons were like all those years ago and gaining an insight like that is worth a great deal. So please treat this book with great respect." And then she put it on one of the shelves by the door.'

'Now think carefully,' I said. 'Did Bob Thompson appear just after that?'

'Now I've gone over it again,' said Izzy, 'I think maybe he did. Maybe a minute later? We'd moved on to something else.'

'Was the classroom door open?' I said.

'Er, yes, I think Muddy left it ajar,' said Izzy.

I sat back against the pillows. 'That's it, then. We've pieced together what the two of you witnessed separately, and we've got an answer. I now know that Bob Thompson had a motive to steal the book. I can see how he made a mistake and thought it was a very valuable item.'

'How?' said Muddy.

Have you worked it out too?

'Bob Thompson was sent by Mrs McEwan to deliver a message to Mrs Penzler,' I said.

'Yes,' said Izzy, 'something to do with paperwork that was due to arrive, now I think about it.'

'So off goes Bob to our classroom,' I said. 'He arrives in the corridor, outside the classroom, just as Mrs Penzler finishes talking about the book. Purely by chance, he hears her as she gets to the bit where she says, "It will give you a feel for what lessons were like all those years ago, and gaining an insight like that is worth a great deal".'

'Or words to that effect,' said Izzy. 'I said I can't be sure.'

'Yes, or words to that effect,' I said. 'But the point is, he only hears the last part. He hears, "that is worth a great deal" and the bit that comes afterwards. He thinks there's now a very valuable old book sitting on those shelves.

'So he waits a minute or two, out in the corridor. That's in case anyone realises he's overheard. He comes into the class and delivers his message and he probably takes a quick look at the shelf too. *How can I get it?* he wonders to himself. He's seen that the donations for the Winter Fayre are also on those shelves and that gives him an idea.

'Enter Bob Thompson, Mr Nice Guy. He volunteers to

help with the Winter Fayre. *I'll go in there tomorrow,* he thinks, *and I'll accidentally on purpose pick up the book with the shirts and bric-a-brac.* The problem is, someone beats him to it. Whatsisface from Mr Nailshott's class really *does* pick up the book, thinking it's for the Fayre. When Bob arrives, after lunch, the donations have gone, and he has to go away empty handed.

'*But all is not lost*, he thinks. *I can retrieve the book from among the donations later today or – if I don't have a chance to do that – at the Fayre itself.* By the end of school today, he still hasn't found it. So what does he do? He spends the whole fair carrying people's bags for them. And quietly taking a peek inside when they're not looking. Exactly when and how he located the book, we don't know. But he'd definitely found it by the end of the Fayre, because at that point he turned back into the miserable, ill-tempered bully he normally is. He now has the book, safely under lock and key, probably, thinking it's worth a small fortune.'

'Right!' cried Muddy. 'First thing tomorrow, we go and talk to Mrs Penzler and she and the Head can have a quiet word with him.'

'That won't do any good,' said Izzy. 'We don't have proof. Correct, Saxby?'

'Correct,' I agreed. 'He could deny he had anything to do with the book and unless we could point to where

175

he's hidden it, which we can't, then we're stuck. No, we need to be clever about this. We need *him* to produce it for *us*.'

'How on earth do we do that?' asked Muddy.

'First things first,' I said. 'Izzy, could you check the online auction and second-hand book sites? See if Mrs Penzler's book is listed anywhere.'

'I'm ahead of you once again,' said Izzy, with just a hint of a laugh. 'I've been monitoring them since the book went missing. Nothing's turned up.'

'Good,' I said. 'That means he's opted for trying to sell the book as quietly as possible. Am I right in thinking Bob Thompson is on the school football team?'

'Yes, I think so,' said Muddy. 'Why?'

'It's football practice after school tomorrow,' I said. 'Which gives us the perfect opportunity to spring our trap.'

CHAPTER FIVE

THE FOLLOWING MORNING, I WAS feeling slightly better. However, I was still dripping snot all over the place and *WHA-CHOOOOOOO*-ing as badly as ever, so I was off school again.

I waited all day for news. I watched that patch of sky outside my window growing brighter, then duller as the day wore on. I picked up half a dozen books, but I couldn't stop my attention wandering. I had a go at sorting out the hideous mess in my wardrobe, but I gave up almost as soon as I started.

It was just gone half past five in the afternoon when Muddy and Izzy arrived. They were almost bursting with excitement.

'It worked?' I asked.

'It worked *perfectly*,' said Muddy.

'We told Mrs Penzler about your plan,' said Izzy. 'She came with us to Rogers and Rogers, straight after school, while Bob Thompson was still at football practice.'

'How did you know he'd go there? And today?' said Muddy.

'He'd want to sell it as soon as possible,' I said. 'This afternoon was his first opportunity. Rogers and Rogers would have been shut by the time he got hold of the book at the Winter Fayre yesterday. And where else would someone so eager to cash in go? Rogers and Rogers is the only second-hand bookdealer in town.'

'You should have seen his face!' said Izzy. 'The three of us just came out from behind a bookshelf. He couldn't believe his eyes!'

'Mrs Penzler has her book back,' said Muddy, 'and Bob Thompson has an appointment with the Head.'

I slapped my hands together with glee. Which set off my cough. Which started me sneezing. Once I'd calmed down a bit, Izzy handed me a pocket-sized photo.

'We thought you might like this,' she said , smiling.

It showed Izzy, Muddy and Mrs Penzler standing beside the shop assistant at Rogers and Rogers. Mrs Penzler had her book in one hand and Bob Thompson's collar in the other. He looked as if he'd been smacked in the face with a nasty shock.

Mrs Penzler had signed the picture in marker pen. Just above her signature she'd written, *Thank you, Saxby.*

I took a drawing pin and stuck the photo to the corkboard above my desk. Every time I looked at it, it made me laugh.

WHA-CHOOOOOOOOOOO!

Case closed.

SAXBY SMART
PRIVATE DETECTIVE

Coming Soon . . .

SAXBY SMART'S

DETECTIVE
HANDBOOK

Don't know a red herring from a fishy tale?

Find out how to be a great detective, like Saxby!
Get the low-down on the sharpest minds of fictional
detectives as well as how real detectives work.
Learn logical thinking, codes, crime-speak
as well as all the gadgets, tricks and traps for
gathering evidence to catch the criminal!

Packed with puzzles, top tips and know-how,
it's everything you need to be as great
a detective as Saxby Smart!

SAXBY SMART
PRIVATE DETECTIVE

Be the sleuth yourself and crack all the cases!

In each story Saxby Smart – schoolboy detective – gives you, the reader, clues which help solve the mystery. Are you 'smart' enough to find the answers?

The **Curse** of the **Ancient** **Mask**

A mysterious curse, suspicious sabotage of a school competition, and a very unpleasant relative all conspire to puzzle Saxby Smart, schoolboy private detective.

Stories include: *The Curse of the Ancient Mask*, *The Mark of the Purple Homework* and *The Clasp of Doom*.

The Fangs of the Dragon

A string of break-ins where nothing is stolen, a rare comic book snatched from an undamaged safe, and clues apparently leading to a hidden treasure – Saxby solves three more challenging crimes.

Stories include: *The Fangs of the Dragon*, *The Tomb of Death* and *The Treasure of Dead Man's Lane*.

The Pirate's Blood

A bloody handprint inside a museum case containing pirate treasure, a classmate with a mysterious secret, and a strange case of arson in a bookshop require Saxby's expert help.

Stories include: *The Pirate's Blood*, *The Mystery of Mary Rogers* and *The Lunchbox of Notre Dame*.

The Hangman's Lair

A terrifying visit to the Hangman's Lair to recover stolen money, a serious threat of blackmail, and a mystery surrounding a stranger's unearthly powers test Saxby to the limit in this set of case files!

Stories include: *The Hangman's Lair, Diary of Fear* and *Whispers from the Dead*.

The Eye of the Serpent

A valuable work of art vanishes into thin air, a notorious crook returns from the dead, and there's an eerie case of stolen identity . . . Time to call in Saxby Smart!

Stories include: *The Eye of the Serpent, The Ghost at the Window, The Stranger in the Mirror*.

Five Seconds to Doomsday

Saxby's arch-enemy plots his ultimate revenge, video games vanish off a truck, and the school office is the target of an apparently pointless robbery. What's really going on?

Stories include: *Five Seconds to Doomsday*, *March of the Zombies* and *The Shattered Box*.

The Poisoned Arrow

Everything's backwards! Saxby must stop a sinister crime before it happens, prove the innocence of a suspect who says they are guilty, and outcheat a team on a school quiz!

Stories include: *The Poisoned Arrow*, *The Nightmare of Room 9B*, *The Final Problem*.

SAXBY SMART
PRIVATE DETECTIVE

www.saxbysmart.co.uk

Featuring an exclusive
online mystery to solve!

Plus:
Saxby Newsletter
Competitions
Ask the Author
Book Disguisers
Writing Tips
and much more!